M000014753

PENGUIN BOOKS

AFTER THE HANGING AND OTHER STORIES

O.V. Vijayan was born in 1930 in Palghat, Kerala. The son of a police officer, he grew up in a camp of armed constabulary commanded by his father. He had no formal schooling till the age of twelve and spent this period at home reading fairy-tales. In 1954 he took a Master's degree in English Literature from Madras University and then taught for a while, before becoming a political cartoonist. His cartoons have appeared in the *Hindu*, the *Statesman*, the *Mathrubhoomi* and the *Far Eastern Economic Review*. He has also published, in Malayalam, three novels, three novellas, five collections of stories and several books of political essays. One of his novels, *The Saga of Dharmapuri*, has been published in English translation by Penguin.

O.V. Vijayan lives in New Delhi.

O.V. VIJAYAN

After the Hanging
and Other Stories

Translated from the Malayalam by the author

PENGUIN BOOKS

Penguin Books (India) Limited, 72-B Himalaya House, 23 Kasturba Gandhi Marg, New Delhi - 110 001, India
Penguin Books Ltd, Harmondsworth, Middlesex, England
Viking Penguin Inc., 40 West 23rd Street, New York, N.Y. 10010. U.S.A.
Penguin Books Australia Ltd, Ringwood, Victoria, Australia
Penguin Books Canada Ltd, 2801 John Street, Markham, Ontario, Canada L3R 1B4
Penguin Books (N.Z.) Ltd, 182-190 Wairau Road, Auckland 10, New Zealand

First published by Penguin Books India 1989

These stories were originally published in the Malayalam in collections brought out by the SPCS, Kottayam, and DC Books, Kottayam.

Page Layouts at Macro Graphics
Made and printed in India by Ananda Offset Private Ltd, Calcutta

To my countryside,
To my childhood

Contents

Author's Note

These stories span a period of over twenty-five years. The first stories in the collection (though chronologically speaking these aren't the early stories I wrote, which were fantasies and romances — these appear in the second sectioı in this arrangement) are concerned with power and terror, occasioned by India's brief experience of the Emergency. Later stories overcome this obsession and explore the need to flow along with life, in a stream of the spirit. The last set of stories are diversions that briefly engaged my attention.

Malayalam is a language that is full of terms of respectful address that are still used by younger people when referring to their elders. Thus achchan (lit. meaning: elder brother), achchi (elder sister), ettan (elder brother), appan (father), and amma (mother) can all be used either literally or as honorifics.

O.V. Vijayan

New Delhi
April 1989

ALLEGORIES OF POWER

The Wart

This was once my garden, the garden I had tended, but today its giant grasses dwarf me. I cower amidst them listening to the awesome rumble of the spiders' chariots, awaiting the wind that will lift me on its brown wave of dust and leaves, and speak to you my brother in the far generations. My time drains away, and I have sinned the sin of the gentle and the pious, and so must make amends. I must communicate... I go back to the wart, drawn to revisit my sin. My sense of time fails me, I cannot recall with any measure of certainty when it all began; it is just as well, because through this story runs a perennial truth whose beginnings go back beyond the times we have known. I remember my wife Suma discovering the wart, tiny as a seed, below my lower lip. I remember, too, the surgeon who said he could cut it away, and how I declined, because my people had never needed surgery—all their healing came from the riverside and the mountain slopes, whose tender shooted specifics were revealed to them by the sage Dhanvantari, the Lord of Health. Generations of my people had meditated on this seer with trust, and I could see no other path for me either. This was my sin, and this now my moment of unburdening...

*

I remember the morning when my razor blade nicked the wart, which bled a little. Suma thought it was a mole, a sign of luck, and it seemed to excite her while we made love. It was many days later, in bed one night, that she asked, 'Do you think this is contagious?'

'I don't,' I said. 'It's just a wart.'

'I was wondering...'

'I'm positive it isn't.'

'Still it is better to remove it. We ought to be telling Aechchu Menon.'

We forgot the conversation. Aechchu Menon was the young surgeon whose clinic was six or seven miles away. He lived close by, a mere mile if you took the bridle path over the hill and the stretch of paddy, but quite some distance by road. I could walk over to his house, but felt reluctant. I was confident that my body, the child of gentle generations, would get back its wholeness through the benediction of leaf and root. In my house there was a crypt-like chamber where much wisdom was stored, inscribed on palm leaves; there, one day, I searched for the cure which would rid me of my excrescence. Guided by the principles the sage Dhanvantari had laid down I walked towards the stream beside which were the dense herbal beds. I plucked the leaves and roots I needed and brought them home.

When Suma saw the green pulp of the medicament over the wart, she said, 'I'd rather you got it cut away.'

Unni, my eight-year-old, overheard her and seemed upset. I drew him close.

'Don't cut it away,' he said.

'Why do you say that?' I asked.

'It will hurt.'

'As you wish,' I said, and smiled. 'We shall try these medicaments.'

These snatches of memory come alive without sequence...

The wart grew large, with a glistening scab around its stem. One night, while making love, I found Suma reluctant and her orgasm impersonal. She lay with her eyes closed and seemed far away. Something told me that she had made love not to me but to my other self, the one without the wart, an adulterous fantasy which made me despair. I sought to get back to her with a show of concern.

'Suma,' I said, 'are you not well?'

'I'm all right,' she said. 'Just tired.'

'Shall we tell Aechchu Menon?'

'There is no need.'

'Shall I give you one of my potions?'

'No,' she said, and turned away, a gesture the import of which I had no desire to understand. However these bouts of distemper passed, and I revived... Ours was a country mansion, a granary fortress a hundred years old. Our estate had dwindled, but there was enough to ensure a life of leisure and contemplation. I did not know the extent of the lands nor how much grain they yielded, but Chaaththan, the head serf, kept count of things for me as had his father for mine. Suma disapproved of this, complaining often of my ineptitude, but I would tell her that

Chaaththan knew better. Everyday I would rise early and bathe, say my beads, and sit down to spin. Unni would soon be off to school and Suma to the kitchen; when I had spun for the day, I would wander over the extensive lands that lay around our house, taking in its compassionate noontide, its gentle browning of leaves, its bird whistles and the ancestral camaraderie of its snakes. Towards the far south of the compound was the giant banyan and the barren patch where my fathers had been cremated. Here I would sit and marvel; soon it would be time to eat and then to lie down for a little sleep in the afternoon. In the evening I would take Unni for a long walk which ended in the temple of Shiva, where the priest kept for Unni his share of the consecrated offering, the palm sugar, fruit and coconut. Thus were my days spent in peace. During one such visit to the temple, Unni stood for a long while before the idol, his eyes closed and palms joined. He opened his eyes when the old priest came up with the offering and tapped him on his shoulder.

'Shall we watch the water-fowl?' I asked as we stepped out of the temple.

'Yes,' Unni said.

This was another ritual of ours, a secret covenant; we would sit on the stone steps of the temple tank, their granite sunset-warm, and the face of water mystic, the migrant water-fowl searing furrows of phosphorescence across it. Today, as usual, we were alone.

We heard the last gongs from the temple; the sanctum was being closed. Unni had lain on the stone, his head on my lap and was soon asleep in the gentle tank breezes. I let him sleep on; the moon had risen when he got up, and the mist was falling. On our way back I asked him, 'Unni, you prayed long today. What did you ask the Lord?'

'To make me a good child,' he said.

'And what else?'

'Well,' he said, 'that's a secret.'

'It doesn't have to be a secret, Unni. What's it?'

'I shouldn't tell it to anyone, or it won't come true.'

'Not really,' I coaxed him. 'It doesn't always have to be so.'

'Well then,' he said, 'I asked the Lord to take your wart away.'

Involuntarily I felt below my lower lip. The wart had grown, its hem of ooze become wider. When we got home, Suma said reproachfully, 'You've kept the child out in the cold so long. The mist is condensing.'

The next evening Unni complained of a sore throat. Suma did not fail to remind me of my negligence.

'Suma,' I said, 'children do catch these colds. A little soup of pepper should make him all right.'

'I suppose you would like the cold to become a fever.'

'What do you want me to do?'

'Can't you show him to a doctor?'

I didn't have a car, and were I to walk Unni all the way to Aechchu Menon's house in the evening, surely his cold would get worse, for it would be well past sundown by the time the doctor returned home and the mist would be falling thick over the hill. There were of course the herbs, but Suma was insistent.

'Let the child stay home,' I said. 'I can go and get the medicine from the doctor.'

'Forget it,' Suma said. 'I'll make the pepper water.'

'But Suma,' I pleaded, 'this is too trivial an illness to call the doctor over.'

'Who's arguing? If that's the way you feel, you don't have to call him.'

She spoke with sullen vehemence; silently I set off for the doctor's house. I waded across the stream, and reaching the hilltop, stood awhile to breathe in the free breezes; the sun had set and the sky was lit with a scarlet afterglow. The village was quiet, its winds free; the hill stood like the incarnate Shiva, and the birds flitted against the red, wind-blown clouds that were his matted locks. But soon, though I did not know it then, amidst these hills and sunsets I would be enslaved by fear and my sorrow imprisoned without communion. To you who watch the rise of the hill and the calm of the sunset, I say this: fear will return to hunt again amid the trees of the hillside, which is why these brief moments of communing are precious... As I went downhill I felt the wart with a new sense of foreboding.

Aechchu Menon was home.

'I finished early today,' he said.

I sat uneasily in a chair in front of him. The young doctor made me conscious of my crumbling manor and my ignorance; he was the son of a family of parvenus, the first man in our part of the country to have mastered the medicine of the English.

'Doctor,' I said, 'Unni has a cold.'

'A cold? That's nothing to be upset about,' he said with a smile. 'I hope he isn't running a fever.'

'No.'

Aechchu Menon went into an ante room, and returned with a strip of packaged pills. I took the pills from him and slipped them into my pocket and said hesitantly, 'You must pardon me if I cause you inconvenience, but it's only because of Suma's insistence. Could you come home?'

'Certainly. We'll drive down.'

I felt guilty about the drive in particular, because unlike the trek over the hill and across the paddies, the road was a long detour.

Soon we were on our way. Suma met us at the door when we arrived. She apologized to the doctor, and he mumbled a pleasantry. He followed Suma into the bedroom and I went in after. Unni lay under a blanket. He woke up and smiled at us.

'That's a naughty child,' Aechchu Menon said. 'Did you play about in the water?'

'No,' said Unni, 'I just sat watching the water-fowl.'

'It was the mist,' said Suma. I sensed the secret bitterness in her voice. Aechchu Menon laughed.

'My kinsman here,' he said, bantering, 'believes in remedies of rain and dew.'

Words rose within me only to ebb away; what could I say about the gentle realm of leaf and root, of the secret covenant between father and son who listen to the gongs of Shiva and watch the water-fowl streak through the dusking water?

Unni had fever that night. The fever lasted five days; in his fever, he threw his arms around me and said, 'Father, you won't let them cut up your face, will you?'

'Why do you keep thinking of it, son?'

'I'm afraid.'

'If it makes you afraid, we shall not let them operate.'

'We shall get medicine from the hillside.'

'We'll do that, little one. Now go to sleep.'

Today I recall my words in sorrow, and know, my son, wherein I failed you. You were pure and young, ignorant of the ways of the microbe; I ought to have armed you with that knowledge...

Suma forbade me nursing Unni. 'Stay away,' she said. 'Do you want the child to catch the disease?'

My hand rose to my wart, it was sticky with ooze. I withdrew to the bath and washed the ooze away, then I looked in the mirror. The wart had grown to the size of a gooseberry. Unni got well in a fortnight. Aechchu Menon visited him every day during his illness, and even after he recovered, made it a practice to visit us and enquire after the child. The wart was now growing faster. One night I woke in great pain. The ducts of the wart had given way; there was the sense of an enormous slush, like the yellow ooze of riven rocks. I felt the wart and realized that it had grown alarmingly. When it was morning I made my way to the hillside and plucked the leaves I needed, pulled out the rarest of roots, and ground them together into medicament invoking the grace of Dhanvantari. But now the wart seemed to suck in the very medicament, to feed on it and grow. Soon it grew to the size of a lemon. If I dropped my gaze, I could see its shadowy contours; the pace of its growth quickened. I realized too that though Aechchu Menon kept visiting us he talked of the wart no more.

Imperceptibly a change came over my relations with people. It was a curious idler first, a man I encountered in the village library, who stared hard at me; then another and another and another, until I found myself driven gently but relentlessly into a prison of their awareness of me. Still I could have carried the wart, now as big as a tomato, in the hammock of my lip, and trudged to the hospital in the town, but in my way was all that my forbears and I had lived by. Suma began to stop my son coming near me. 'It's a disease,' she told Unni. 'A contagion.'

I chose not to hear my son's reply, the strength for that knowing had gone from me, and slowly I climbed up to the panelled attic, which would henceforth be my home... One night in the attic, lying on an ancient cot of rosewood, I communed with the ancestral shades around me. *My fathers,* I said, *these riversides and mountain slopes bear witness to your freedom, and yet what has befallen me, your son? You bequeathed to me the precious palm leaf with its arcana of healing, and yet why have these leaves and roots failed to prevail over this invading spore?* In the aged panelling, and in the walls of our sprawling home, they awoke and listened and answered me with a great tide of sadness.

I had lain long thus in the stream of my fathers, when I was aware of someone moving stealthily through the attic's dark. It was Suma! I rose and moved towards her. She had an earthen pot in her hands. 'Take this,' she said.

I took the cold bowl from her and smelt the aroma of Dhanvantari's medicaments.

'Merciful Lord,' I said.

'I got them from the *vaidyan*. This is his prescription. Take it.'

A multitude of beneficent things were within me, they lit me with cool and gentle lights; so she had gone to the *vaidyan* despite her awe of the apothecary, she had come up to the attic overcoming her revulsion of the giant carbuncle that sat on my lip. I threw my arms around her; she did not resist, but when I bent over to kiss her, she said, 'We should not. It is not for me, but for our son that I deny you so.'

'Suma,' I said, 'this is no contagion. This is a wart.'

'It's a wart,' she said.

'Come,' I said.

She stood reluctant in the dark, then forbade me gently. When I took her face in my palms, her cheeks were wet.

'Oh, god,' I said.

With a sob she came down on her knees, and unable to lift her up, I sat down beside her.

'Unni does not eat,' she said. 'He's pining away.'

Here my memories fade, it is merciful they do; I remember that unspoken words moved on like a procession of termites from me to her and from us to our child, until the termite tracks were deserted and there was nothing but the attic's dark and the earthen bowl which held Dhanvantari's gentle medicament. I sat awhile and gazed into the vessel until I was overcome again by weariness and sleep. I woke again, the moon had risen in the window. The ancestral shades on my walls were now vibrant. I rose and paced my prison with the righteousness of my fathers. It was then that the moon lit up an ancient razor's edge. My great uncle Koppunni had himself shaved with this blade and here amid derelict artifacts it had lain these long years. The knife blazed now, and I remembered my great uncle. We are a gentle and pious people, but our genealogy is punctuated by proud and regal ancestors as well. Koppunni Nair was one such. He strode the hillside in the rain, and grew to power in the green nutrients of the recurring seasons. I could see him now as he used to sit before the serf-barber for the ritual tonsure; this was the knife, on no other did the barber use it; it cleansed the scalp round his tuft and the base of his phallus, so that he was shorn anew into nakedness and could romp down the hillsides to seek out wedded matrons and sow in them the seeds of bastard sovereignty — and the children, in the incestuous unknowing of their ancestry, would chase and mate with one another. The wildness of the knife roused me, and I went to the shelf in the panelling and picked it up. It glistened in the moon. I did not know what followed; perhaps the knife and its power compelled me. The suicidal violence of my great uncle welled up within me along with the futile resistance of the gentle and the pious, and in that great mingling I held the wart with my left hand and with the right drew the knife along its stem.

*

The swoon must have lasted months. When I came to my senses it was another season in the skylight. Instinctively, I raised my hand to feel the wart. There it was, defiant and invincible, the size of a coconut, and around it, like stalagmite or coral, glistened scab and fester.

Chaaththan came up to the attic. 'We had given you up, master.'

'Chaaththan!'

'What is it, my master?'

I lay awhile in silence, to regain my voice.

'How long,' I asked at last, 'did the swoon last?'

'Three months, master.'

In the corner of the attic I saw heaps of drying herbs, and smelled their gentle aroma.

'Have you been nursing me with these?' I asked.

'You've taught me to minister thus, my master.'

'Chaaththan!'

'Yes, my master?'

The words as they formed inside me sounded portentous. I held them back awhile, then spoke them trembling.

'Chaaththan,' I asked, 'where is Unni?'

Chaaththan did not reply. He slowly walked to a cupboard in a corner, and from it took a sealed letter.

'Here, master,' he said, 'this is the mistress's letter.'

'The mistress's letter?' I repeated, incredulously.

Chaaththan looked away and was silent; I tore open the cover and read; in disbelief I skated back and forth over rounded script. *I am going,* she had written. *You and I can only console ourselves that such is our destiny. I am going away to a far country with Aechchu Menon. I shall put no more in words, lest it cause you more pain. I ask your forgiveness, so does he... Unni will live in my ancestral home, my brothers will look after him. Afflicted as you are, I shall not burden you with his care...'*

Darkness descended on my eyes, and as they cleared, I felt the wart twitch... On the walls the ancestral shades had fallen quiet. I looked for Koppunni Nair's knife, but it was nowhere to be found..

*

Slowly, like the fading and becoming of seasons, I experienced a new quiet and a new acceptance. I came down from the attic, and every day at dawn I walked over the grass in the garden wet with the night's dew. Before the sun was up Chaaththan would come to me with the goings-on in the fields and the orchards, and do the reckoning. After that his young sister-in-law would bring in the milk, steam a banana for my breakfast, cook for the day, and depart. Sometimes at night, Chaaththan would come up to find out how I was. That was the last thing for the day, after which I was left alone with the wart. The old house sprawled, enormous and cheerless, its rooms inaccessible like far provinces, where the vermin multiplied and broke the sleep of my fathers with malefic noises... The wart grew.

Chaaththan's concern was now slackening, and Naani, the sister-in-law, began to play truant. I questioned her when she turned up after one of her absences. After much insistence she answered, 'There was work at home.'

It was folly to question her further, it was folly for me to demand anything, I told myself. I remembered Suma's great reluctance, the freezing love play, the nights which gave us the final knowledge of our alienation. What might she be doing at this moment? The sun was climbing high, and soon it would be noon, when in the land of her refuge it would perhaps be midnight. Starting out of her sleep now, she would make love again; I sensed the wet of her lips, the felt and unseen breasts, the thighs, and the fair disc of the belly rising to meet the man's desire again and again. And then the interminable sleep, the interminable nakedness. I must have sat unmoving for a long while, all this smouldering and dying within me. Naani had left hours earlier.

All day long I chased Suma's memory with horrendous lust. As the night advanced I quietened, and in its place came a great tenderness for my son, and like a little boy, I cried myself to sleep... Early the next morning, I walked out of my compound gate and waded into the stream. There were no other bathers, nor any people in sight. I stood naked in the flowing water. Only my face had been claimed by the wart, my body was still mine, and limb by limb, it was sturdy and beautiful.

The wart was now a slab of meat. I felt the burden within as well; in vain I sought a place in my mind where I could rest it awhile. Thus I went one day to the boundary fence, beyond which lay the serfs's tenements. It was noon already, and I had not eaten since morning. I called out for Naani. She came to the fence.

'Has Chaaththan gone to the fields?' I asked her.

'Yes, my master.'

Naani looked hard at the wart.

'My master,' she said, 'it has grown big.'

We stood on either side of the fence, close to each other.

Then I asked her, 'Naani, why have you stopped coming?'

'The chores at home,' she answered without conviction.

We fell silent again.

'Naani,' I said, 'did Chaaththan stop you from coming?'

'Yes,' she mumbled.

'Did he say it was contagious?'

Again, sadly, she nodded.

Naani was young, and beautiful in the manner of aboriginal women, her limbs strong and her skin the deep colour of honey, her lips black and glistening a healthy wet, windblown ringlets about the temples, the hair of an ancient race. Then, as I stood looking at her, the wart's crust cracked and there was a great gush of ooze. Paralyzed, I stood by the fence.

On an impulse Naani pulled off her upper cloth and held it towards me.

'Take this, my master,' she said, 'and wipe the pus away.'

I took the proffered cloth, her bared breasts now basked in the sun. I wiped the ooze with my fingers and returned her cloth unsoiled.

'Naani.'

'Yes, my master?'

'Will you come?'

She did not reply.

'Naani.'

'Yes, my master?'

Silence again.

'Naani.'

'Yes, my master?'

'Naani,' I asked again, 'will you come to work?'

Quietly she said, 'I shall.'

I lumbered back into the house and sat behind a fretted casement and waited. I did not have to wait long; I saw her crossing the yard. She entered the room uncertainly and stood before me.

'Naani.'

'Yes, my master?'

'Are you repelled?'

I bent my head and averted my gaze. She did not reply.

'My master,' she asked, 'when is the mistress coming back?'

'She is not coming back.'

Naani asked me nothing more; her eyes wandered about the room; and soon she was aware of nothing but the little things, the cobwebs, the drying peel of bananas, the crumpled ball of paper in the corner. She picked up a broom and began to sweep.

'I am back, my master,' she said. 'Be at ease.'

'Naani.'

She leaned the broom on the wall and came over to me. I had no predetermined idea of what I wanted from her, but found myself saying, 'I want to bathe. I want a warm bath.'

She moved into the inner rooms, noiselessly. Soon there rose the scents of medicinal oils warming over the hearth. She came back and said, 'Your bath is ready, my master.'

I walked towards the bath, and she followed me with the oils and the pulp of gram. She entered the bath after me, and began to rub the oils on my hands and legs.

'My master!' said Naani.

I was crying. She pressed my face against her belly, and in my sorrow and dependence I began disrobing her. She pressed me harder against her body's deep honey-hued translucence. I closed my eyes, and behind the shelter of those lids I was whole and handsome again... My eyes closed, I kissed her on her parted lips, my sorrow spilled over her and was spent. The wart twitched.

That night, for the first time in many nights, I slept deep. When I woke up the next morning I found the wart grown inordinately. I could hardly lift my face, and I began walking about the house with my head bent, with the sorrow of a lowly hog. I went to the mirror, and in great pain raised my face to it. As I studied the image, I saw a red slit across the wart, and two black spots. For a moment I was relieved; I thought the wart was suppurating and about to burst.

In this renewed hope, I plucked more leaves and roots and ground them into medicament. When I spread it round the wart, it smarted as it had never before, and I had the uncanny feeling that it was moving and wriggling. When the medicament dried and peeled away, the wart appeared even larger.

About ten days after Naani had given me the bath, it became difficult for me to hold myself up. When she brought me my milk one morning, I was lying crushed by the weight of my face.

'Are you in much pain, my master?' Naani asked.

I made a vain attempt to rise, then gave up and lay down.

'Let me hold you, my master.'

She held me and propped me against the cushions.

'I can't bear this burden anymore,' I said.

She pressed the palm of her hand between her breasts, her eyes closed; I saw her lips move in prayer. After that she disrobed me gently, and keeping her eyes away from my disfigurement , began caressing me. A great desire rose in me, swamping the pain and the burden of the excrescence; I desired Naani to anoint me, desired that we should anoint each other on the cold tiles of the bath. Soon we were covered with Dhanvantara, the ancient unction of the sage, we went down on the floor like twining serpents. Thus does the unfree man seek freedom, in lust; like the condemned prisoner who spends his last moments not on God but mating with empresses in his fantasy. There occurs one moment when someone peeps into your prison cell and tells you he can cut away the tumid flesh; but you turn away to your roots and leaves, like the condemned one to his empresses; the moment slips by, never to occur again... I was about to enter Naani when the wart twitched violently, and I fancied I heard a noise like a fish plummeting into water, and a scream of pain rose from Naani.

Piercing through the pus and scab, an enormous phallus had come out of the wart. I fell away, but felt a miraculous power pulling me up. It was the wart, drilling down beneath my scalp and holding me up in an unseen lasso. I found myself lying on Naani once again, now my face on her pubis. I felt the black phallus rise; the wart took Naani!

I am appalled by the enormity of my sin as I recollect how the wart rose and fell on Naani, taking her to a tumultuous climax, and how I shared the experience with the wart. I had till then considered the wart an alien impurity, but from now I was to know that this thing, which I had fostered with the nutrients of my body and the folly of my piety, was flesh of my flesh. The interminable orgasm drew a deep sleep over me, and when I awoke my limbs had grown cold on the tiles of the bath. I sat up with great effort. The cheerless dusk and the damp tiles depressed me. Then I realized that Naani might catch a chill if she slept long on the floor.

'Naani, 'I said, shaking her, 'wake up. You'll freeze. '

The violence of the orgasm had apparently exhausted her, and, lips slack, thighs apart, the palms of her hands resting on her breasts, and blood and ooze drying below her navel, Naani slept. Then once again the wart's lust became mine. My senses spun, and I drifted into a swoon.

It must have lasted many days; it was a strong stench that awakened me. I sat up and looked at Naani; nothing had changed in the tableau of rape: the parted lips and thighs, the palms resting on the breasts. I touched her thighs, the flesh had begun to rot, and as I took my hand away, I heard an eerie laugh like the cackle of a woodpecker. I was alone with a corpse and its mortuary odour. The unseen woodpecker laughed again. Fear gave me the energy to rise and move; I went up to the mirror to take a look at the wart. It hung from my lower lip like a sea turtle. The red patch I had seen and which I had mistaken for inflammation and possible decay, now opened up into a mouth, vampire lips drooling spit and pus and the black dots into a pair of eyes, little eyes winking lewdly at me from the mirror. The lips moved now and once again I heard the spectral cackle of the woodpecker. As I listened intently the cackle defined itself into words of frenzied and obscene abuse.

Now the last spaces of my freedom vanished, the spaces I had conjured with my desperate lust. The prison closed round me, and I was left alone with the wart, my prison warden. And now the wart began to communicate to me its commands and helplessly I obeyed. Whenever I failed to decipher the woodpecker's cackle, the wart squirted pus on me. With patient industry I trained myself for this new listening, and soon I was lost to the speech of free men. Tugging with secret reins at my mind, the wart now put me to work. There was a lumber room on top and one night the wart commanded me to climb up there. It was pitch dark inside, but pointers of a denser darkness led me on. Disturbed out of their ancient trances, tarantulas spiralled dizzily up my legs and down and away. The wart directed me to rummage in the junk. I thrust my fingers amid sodden and rusted things, amid hidden venoms, until at last I touched cold steel. It was Koppunni Nair's razor. I could not understand how it had got up here. The wart directed me to pick it up. We climbed down from the lumber room with the weapon.

There was a pall of mist outside, the moonlight full of disquiet. I remember my fingers tightening round the handle, I remember the first paces of a murderous sleepwalk; then the long swoon took over. When I awoke the knife was still in my hand, and I was covered with black and red stains. The wart asked me to get up: we walked to the old well. It directed me to fling the knife into the well. As the knife shot through to the depths and pierced the deep lens of water, I sent up a prayer to my ancestors. The wart crouched and listened, and desecrated my prayer with foul abuse. I sought consolation in the knowledge that the wart was still my excrescence, that it had once been a lowly knot of ducts on my lip. At that the woodpecker's cackle spoke, not in my ear but within my mind, *you transgress the law.*

Wherein do I transgress? I asked.

Memory, the wart said. *Memory is a crime against history.*

I spoke with sadness into my mind, *You were born of my flesh. Why did you take away my freedom, the freedom of the one who gave you your being?*

The wart writhed in great rage, and flung searing javelins of pain into my bloodstream.

Spare me, spare me, I cried out.

When you speak to me hereafter, the wart said, *you must call me your brother.*

Brother, I said.

Not that way, the wart said.

Teach me how, I said.

In this manner, the wart said. It gave me the knowledge of willing servitude. Brotherhood was a word of freedom, but from now on, words would change, and so would everything that came from the sacred grottos of the mind.

That night the wart ordered me to the gate of our manor; from some distance away came the sound of people. There were policemen with red berets on the rampage. I remembered the knife and the blood on my palms; a great distress came over me, and I asked the wart. *Where is my loyal serf, and where is his wife?*

You need not know, the wart said severely.

I need not, I repeated. *Brother,* I called the wart, in a snivelling of the mind. I accepted my sovereign.

I knew the wart smiled. *Good,* it said. *It's time to feed. Move on to the bath.*

The stench in the bath had grown so dense that it was the colour of the moss of death, a death unredeemed by rebirth. I dragged myself inside. The wart asked me to lie down on Naani's corpse once again for a funereal mating. It kissed the black parted lips, then I heard a noise like the snip-snipping of barber's scissors. Naani's lips vanished, I knew the acid taste of rot. A skeletal grin flashed where the lips had been, soon the eyes and cheeks and nose disappeared, and then there was a noise of the crushing of bones and of their softening in the chemistry of spit, followed by the monotonous slurping of treacle. When it was over, I was given the command to rise.

I stood on the tiles of the bath. Naani lay headless at my feet, her thighs apart and her hands folded over swollen nipples. Like a delicate pall over her body was the patina of mould. From all over her underbelly seeped fearsome secretions, while within her womb grew the foetus of death.

To the mirror now, the wart said. Now I saw the wart had sprouted supple tendrils, hands of the wart!

God, I said.

No sooner had I uttered that word, the javelins burned through my blood and my endurance gone, I cried out in supplication, *Brother, brother*! The javelins were called back.

Brother, my just and all-powerful brother! I chanted. The wart was pleased.

With its new grown hands the wart began to hunt; it gave chase to the wild cats and bandicoots, from the lumber rooms it caught bats and preyed on them. Naani's headless corpse had by now become a frothing, bubbling puddle. The wart mated with it again and again.

One night my thoughts dwelt on Suma and Unni with an intensity I had never before experienced. I sought them in the scalding darkness of my sorrow. I floundered and fell and wept. The wart listened. Once in every man's lifetime, once perhaps, his sorrow rises to enormity, and like the will of a king, sweeps away everything before it. This was the moment of my grief and power. The wart stood by and watched. When my lamenting subsided, I waited for the punishing javelins. They never came. The stench too had gone; after one last union the wart had licked up the puddle with great gluttony. The javelins had not come in my moment of insubordination, but I was to be punished yet; all nutrients were withheld from my bloodstream. Within me grew a hunger like an unseen fire that licks through mountain crevices. I began to dwindle, even as the wart grew by leaps and bounds; I became a mere appendage. Then one day the wart battered down the doors of my chamber of palm leaf manuscripts and sought the arcana of Dhanvantari. It was lost in study for a while, after which it went out to the hillside for leaves and roots. I watched it make the medicament and lay it thick around the stem of my diminutive body. There was a searing pain, followed by numbness and sleep.

I woke amid flaming dandelions, the sun was bright overhead and the wind blew with the aroma of living plants. I realized I was in my garden. I saw an enormous creature roll in from behind the house. The wart! The medicaments had worked, and I had shrivelled and fallen off the wart's great body. There was a weird change in the scale of things, the grass blades were like towers and dragonflies descended on them like airships. I had shrunk to the size of a worm.

The wart rolled about in the garden. The sun climbed to a

blazing noon, then set and rose again. The spiders hunted amid the green. The wart grew and in its growing changed. Its black hide shone. It had legs, great flapping ears, a trunk and tusks. The wart had become an elephant.

Down the hill came a band of Brahmins, and saw the elephant frolicking in the waters of the stream that flowed through my lands.

'A truly majestic elephant,' they said.

'The temple could use him for the procession.'

'Whose elephant is it?'

'Koppunni's.'

'Koppunni was indeed a connoisseur.'

'Look this way, elephant...'

In my worm's voice, thin like a pupal thread, I cried out: *pious brahmins, this is no elephant, this is a microbe. I shall tell you its tale.* But the Brahmins were gone. The wind rose and the dead leaves rustled.

The elephant received the offerings of the temple, the fruit, the palm sugar and the tender fronds of coconut, and on its back glittered the idol of the temple's god. The sorrows of the pious and the gentle were forgotten, and so too the death scent of the merciful woman. But I had my freedom, the freedom of the cast-away. The wart had given me my freedom, the wart, my prison warden. Then like a deluge came the awareness of the living force which fulfilled itself as much in the toxic microbe as it did in the seeds of life. Skies unfolded in my tiny head, and in them shone a benevolent sun.

Om bhoor bhuva swawaha
Tat savitur varenniyam
Bhargo devasya dheemahi
Dheeyo yonah prachotayat
Almighty Light
pervader of the earth and the sky
of the gross and the subtle
illumine my intellect...

Once again, the leaf and the root of the gentle exuberate in the bounty of the Sun.

It was in my folly, my lord God, that I forgot Your perennial becoming. You are the prisoner's door.

The Foetus

Capping the layered darkness of the fortress were domes of bronze, looking from afar like malignant carbuncles. Banyans, their branches arched and held by buttressing roots, stood guard around the fortress like prehistoric spiders. Behind the fortress's walls of cold granite and doors of rosewood lived the Lady, widowed Sovereign of the village. The people seldom saw her, and when after long years she became pregnant, the news of her pregnancy only became known to the village through hesitant chambermaids. At this time fearsome omens manifested themselves in the village, the perennial spring of the temple tank dried up, even as the Lady's womb ceased its bleeding.

The villagers heard the sound of bells and conches at night from the fortress, dark prayers for the foetus. One evening, after the worship, the Priest of the temple implored the Astrologer to cast his cowrie shells.

'O Astrologer,' the Priest said, 'ask the spirits of the planets about this pregnancy.'

They sat down on the smooth clay floor of the temple's verandah, and the Astrologer flung his shells and divined the message of the planets.

'Is it an immaculate conception?' the Priest asked in anxiety. The Astrologer gathered his shells together and flung them again and meditated.

'The planets do not speak,' the Astrologer said. Suddenly there were three young men looming behind him.

'Old man,' their leader said, 'read your shells properly. This is an immaculate conception, and the people need such a reading.'

His voice was menacing, and the Astrologer looked up helplessly.

'Cast your shells again,' the young man said. The Astrologer did so.

'Don't you see it is immaculate?' demanded the young man.

In a weak voice the Astrologer assented, 'I do.'

The young men turned and left the temple. The Priest now asked the Astrologer, 'Do you, in truth?'

'I see nothing.'

On the village common, the three young men gathered with others of their class, scions of the gentry, and their leader spoke to them, 'It is the Foetus of our Sovereign.'

High above, the stars shone in mystic conjunctions, but their message never reached the village; a foetal membrane spread over it like an astral canopy... Three months passed. The Foetus grew within the dark fortress.

*

One morning, the peasants wending their way to work early saw vultures over the wild palm grove of the village, wheeling like a giant eddy of flying reptiles. Rushing to the grove, they found the village drummer lying dead. There were marks of strangulation round his neck, and a gash near his heart; all the blood had been drained away from his body and from where he lay a broad trail of slime stretched towards the village, punctuated with bloody drip. The peasants followed the trail and discovered that it led to the massive gate of the fortress. There they stood hesitant; just then a conch sounded inside the fortress, and the fierce hounds tethered in the kennels howled in spectral relay.

'Let us go away,' counselled an old ploughman, and the peasants went back to work.

The village accepted the death as an inexplicable aberration, and chose to forget it. But the drummer's brother decided to investigate. The next night, in drunken courage, he lay in wait in the palm grove. At midnight, a flurry of nocturnal birds rose with cries of alarm and the brother saw an enormous blob of jelly slithering up the trail, its malefic fluids glistening in the moon. As he watched it, all desire to confront it left him, and he turned and fled. Some distance up the path he stumbled and fell; before he lost his senses, he felt cold and slimy tentacles grip him, and a tiny mouth make incisions on his flesh.

The sunlight woke him; he tottered back home, unsteady, much of his blood drained away.

'Where have you been?' his wife asked. 'And what has happened to you?'

Without answering, he slumped into bed and slept till afternoon. His wife did not question him again. Two nights later the village was woken up by the bleating of terrified goats in the goat-herd's stable. People from the neighbouring huts rushed to the stable with lanterns and torches. In the goat-herd's yard lay a kid, its leg severed. A trail of blood and slime led from the stable to the gate and down the lane.The goat-herd and his neighbours swished their torches in the wind setting them aflame, and followed the trail. Dozing ratsnakes moved aside for the crowd to pass. The little torch-lit procession followed the relentless trail, and presently came to the shut gates of the fortress. Undecided, they lingered before the gate, when, like an occult response, the hounds howled inside the fortress. The villagers turned back, their lips sealed by the omens of the night.

*

Soon the slime drew trails over every lane and footpath. Alongside the trails appeared the marks of hounds' feet and the silent nights were pierced with their howling. The village midwife examined the slime-soaked earth and told the villagers that it was foetal fluid.

In the temple the Priest and the Astrologer conferred.

'O Astrologer,' the Priest said, 'evil stalks the village. What is the being that leaves these trails of slime and death?'

'My inner voice tells me what it is,' the Astrologer said. 'But I dare not say it.'

'Cast your shells and divine it.'

'It is no use, O Priest. The planets are eclipsed in this village.'

The Priest pondered this reply, and said, 'Then let us walk tonight to the next village, and in the temple there, try to read the stars.'

'Yes, we might try.'

The Priest took with him the book of the goddess's litany and they set out to the next village. The temple yard was open, and there they sat and cast the shells.

'My shells touch the spirits of the planets,' the Astrologer said. 'Nothing hides the skies here.'

'The goddess be praised.'

The Astrologer heaped the shells and flung them again and again. On his face appeared a great sadness.

'O Priest,' he said, 'my worst fears are confirmed. It is our Sovereign Lady's foetus. It comes out of the womb and hunts in the night, and goes back into the womb. It is protected by the hounds, and in the hounds dwell the spirits of the Lady's ancestors, spirits of unquenched evil.'

The Priest gasped, and said after an agonized silence, 'This is unnatural, nothing like this has happened in the village before.'

'Far from it, it was happening all the while. For many generations the lords of the fortress had willed their power over us, and this manifests itself in this blob of slime.'

'Are we doomed, O Astrologer?'

The Astrologer smiled and stretched his hand to touch the book of litany. 'Trust this,' he said.

*

But the young scions of the gentry had no book of litany to trust, they trusted their reason, and the exuberance of their bodies, the bodies that hunted and preened and made love. It was with them that the Foetus communed in the mysterious emanations of the night. Soon there were carnivals of youth to celebrate the advent of the Foetus. At the end of these carnivals, the youth would march to the fortress with offerings of goats and roosters and bunches of bananas for the Foetus. They would leave the offerings at the gate; the gate would open at night when the Foetus woke, and the hounds would tug the offerings inside.

The leader of the youth spoke to his flock, 'The Foetus is our new Sovereign, and we are his soldiers. The old order is crumbling.'

In time, the office of the village council was overrun and occupied by the youth. The old councillors, wise elders, were driven away. Soon two portraits adorned the council-hall, one of the Lady, in the carnal fullness of middle age, pregnant, naked. The young men gazed on this in spasms of lust. The other portrait, before which fervent worship was offered, was of a blob of gelatine, turgid and luminescent, with tiny hands and feet. The Foetus!

The lusting and the worship grew like tides of neurosis, they seeped out of the council-hall and engulfed the village.

Yet two old men resisted, with their piety. After the worship was over at the temple one night, the Priest and the Astrologer sat on its deserted verandah and talked into the late hours.

'O Astrologer,' the Priest said, 'there have been deaths in the village.'

'There have always been deaths.'

'There have been, but these are unblessed deaths, deaths of people who had sought refuge in the goddess.'

'What does it betoken?'

'That the goddess hears our prayers no more. She has turned away from us.'

A frenzy seized the Astrologer and agitated his tuft.

'Pray,' he said. 'Pray!'

*

The tributes reached the fortress without interruption, and the Foetus fed on them and rested. For the next two months there were no slime trails in the village. The scions of the gentry grew anxious, and one day marched to the fortress, and assembled at the gate where they chanted an address to the Lady. The dogs howled, but were silenced, and then from the depths of the fortress a voice, husky and seductive, spoke to them, 'What do you desire, my children?'

'O Sovereign!' the leader of the youth replied, 'for the last two months, the Incarnation has not left his trails in the village. We feel orphaned.'

'He slumbers and grows. Have patience.'

'The peasants resist us. Peasant women spurn our desires.'

'The Incarnation has mastered the trails of the night. He broods and grows to master the paths of sunlight. Soon he will come out to lead you.'

A cry of joy rose from the scions, and they said, 'Truly he is our eternal Sovereign, unborn and undying!'

The honeyed voice from the fortress said, 'Go now, my children!'

And it came to pass during the festival bath; the granite steps of the temple tank were packed with women come for the holy dip. They bathed bare-breasted as was the custom, a hundred of them. As the women performed their ablutions, there came to the tank a red palanquin borne by swarthy and bearded men, strangers to the village. They set the palanquin down near the women's bathing *ghat*, and as the bathers watched in panic, the

Foetus tumbled out of the palanquin, and lifted its gaze to the sun. Then it heaved itself up on misshapen limbs, and crouched towards the *ghat* like a crystal tarantula.

'Make way,' the palanquin bearers cried. 'Make way for the Sovereign's bath!'

The women parted on the *ghat*, and the Foetus rolled down the steps and plummeted into the water. It swam about amidst the naked breasts, and gobbled the tame old fishes of the temple tank which drifted towards it in gentle curiosity. The Foetus frolicked in this manner for a while, when suddenly a pregnant woman cried out, 'Help! It has got into me!'

The women rushed to her rescue, but she cried, 'Keep away, or it will kill me.' She sank neck deep and sat on the submerged steps, eyes closed. The bathers stood aside and watched in helpless terror. Then the pregnant woman sank with a shriek of pain into the water and was lost. From the sullied waves the Foetus rose and climbed the steps. It was followed by another, smaller, foetus. Together they crawled towards the palanquin, their trails slushy over the wet earth. The Foetus climbed in, followed by its protégé, and the swarthy men lifted the palanquin and were gone.

As the women raised a lament and beat their bare breasts, the scions of the gentry swooped down on the *ghat*.

'No,' matrons clad in wet sarongs pleaded. 'No, children!'

But the young men plunged into the water, and swam after the women, stripping them in the water and feeling them for signs of pregnancy.

'Desist, my children!' a grandmother cried.

'No!' replied the leader of the youth. 'This is the Sovereign's search. There are no private pregnancies any more.'

The women swam round in distraught circles, and their pursuers came upon them, blind to identity, incestuous.

*

Now the sunlight held no terrors for the unborn eye, the Foetus made daytime sallies into the market place... At the far end of the village, in a forlorn cottage apart from other houses, lived the Insurrectionist, enfeebled by age, the forgotten hero of many sad and passionate uprisings. He was seated one day palavering with peasant partisans, when they felt the glow of day grow suddenly dim, as though someone had drawn a blind. Hiding the light in the doorway was a barrier of risen slime, a mess of marrow and cartilage.

'Look!' the Insurrectionist gasped. 'What manifestation is this?'

'It is the Foetus, comrade,' the peasants said.

The Insurrectionist lived in his cocoon of senility and heroism, he was only dimly aware of the new presence in the village, and was, as a revolutionary materialist, of miracles. The sceptical Incarnation leered; behind it lined up the lesser foetuses, and behind them the human mercenaries. After an unnerving pause the Foetus rolled in, and so did the foetal storm troop. The peasants made an attempt to resist, while the Insurrectionist offered a bland combativeness as if he were duelling with phantoms from his long lost class struggles.

In one swift move the Foetus grabbed the old man's legs and slithered up; the other foetuses did likewise with the peasants, and soon the Insurrectionist and his comrades stood paralyzed, their heads bent under crowns of translucent jelly. With misshapen hands the foetuses now began to massage the men's temples and foreheads, as though rubbing in a lethal unction. *Submit*, said an unspoken and monstrous command, *We vampirize your Revolution, we vampirize your historical memory*. The captives winced in pain. The insistent message went on, *We want your Revolution's full blooded wenches whom we shall deflower for the New Order*.

Decades of legendary battle softened into inane compliance; the partisans' invaded minds soon began signalling back in psychic code, *We follow you, Sovereign; take our Revolution, take our wenches*.

The mesmeric evil had claimed them, and it fanned out through the village like an inexorable seepage... Yet two men, calm in their piety, held out: in the temple, deserted after the day's worship, the Priest asked the Astrologer, 'Tell me, brother, is our servitude perennial?'

'Nothing is perennial, O Pious One.'

'What is to be done?'

'Nothing. The Spirit of Order recuperates.'

*

The Priest tried hard to share the Astrologer's optimism, but what he witnessed the next day at his daughter's school shattered him. His daughter was laid up with fever, and he had gone to the school to ask for leave of absence. Halfway to the school he came upon fleeing school children , who were too tongue-tied to explain their flight; he walked on with great foreboding. He found the school surrounded by the young gentry and the little foetuses. He chanted the litany of the goddess and walked past the encirclement. Chairs and desks lay overturned, and on the teacher's dais the young and comely class teacher lay stretched, her saree torn to shreds and her skirt shoddily rolled up. Nestling between her bared thighs was the Foetus!

'Rape!' the Priest cried, seized with rage. The next instant a bludgeon stunned him, but even as he sank into the blank dark, he chanted the litany in his mind. When he came to his senses there was no sign of the teacher or the Foetus. The gentry too had dispersed. On his neck and temples were abrasions, as though a giant snail or leech had tried to bleed him. The headmaster sat beside him, concerned.

'Sir,' the Priest asked, 'what happened?'

'Nothing,' the headmaster said sleepily. 'Nothing really.'

'The Foetus...'

'Be at peace, O Priest. The Sovereign is kind, and his dynasty has looked after this village for many generations.'

The Priest sat up, the abrasions hurting. 'But tell me, Sir,' he said, 'isn't it unnatural? A foetus slithering in and out of its mother's womb and refusing the grace of birth? Think, Sir, think!'

'Think, think...' the headmaster mumbled in despair, and fainted. The Priest laid his hand on the headmaster's forehead. 'All-powerful goddess,' he said, 'protect us from evil.'

The Priest walked home in a daze. He sat beside his ailing daughter, and said, 'My child, do not go to that school again.' The answer came from one of her class mates who had come visiting, 'But, Sir, there isn't any school any more.'

'There isn't?'

'The school has been closed down, and all instruction forbidden. Lessons have been replaced by slogans, which the gentry will teach us.'

'It can't be,' the Priest said hysterically. 'It can't be!'

'But it has been accomplished. It is the Law, the Foetus's Law.'

'The school closed down!' the Priest muttered.

'That is not all. The Foetus has outlawed childbirth. Henceforth the village will have only foetuses.'

The Priest rose in anger. 'This is violence and intrusion,' he cried. 'I will go to the police and complain. I will go right away.'

The girl laughed sadly. 'There are no police left,' she said.

'It can't be, it can't be! Only the ministers in the capital can send the police away.'

'But, Sir,' she said, 'don't you realize we are an island in time, our destiny come to a halt?'

The Priest beat his head and wept, 'What is it that has come over us?'

'Sorcery.'

*

In that sorcery the Foetus stayed unborn and threatened to go on in perpetuity. So did its foetal following.

Every morning now the Foetus came to the marketplace riding in the red palanquin. Behind it in a greasy phalanx marched the little foetuses, and behind them, chanting slogans, the violent young men of the gentry. Often, the oldest citizen of the village, its only surviving centenarian, brought up the rear of this weird revue. The exercise hastened the old one's terminal illness, and as he lay dying, the Priest visited his home to read him the holy verses.

'O elder,' the Priest said 'must you have put yourself through this exercise?'

'I have no regrets,' the old man replied.

'You, our centenarian, following a mere foetus!'

'Aged disciples have always walked behind young messiahs.'

The Priest shrugged his shoulders and sat down to recite the verses.

'Not that!' the old man protested. The Priest paused uncomprehending. The old man went on, 'We have overcome this book. If you want to do me a good turn, call in the little foetuses, and implore them to chant me the Sovereign's slogans while I die.'

Hardly had the old man finished speaking, when the red palanquin disgorged its gelatinous content into the hut. The Foetus filled the doorway, and once again the Unborn Thing and the goddess's Priest stood facing each other. In the yard the little foetuses crowded together like an unharvested bubonic crop. The Foetus took slow, determined steps towards the Priest, its fore-limbs raised menacingly. The Priest opened the book, the verses came out of him, resonant. Like a predator closing its mandibles, the Foetus lowered its hands. Chanting ceaselessly, the Priest walked past the Foetus, and past the foetal host outside.

In great agitation he reached the sanctuary of the temple, where the Astrologer rested, leaning on a carved pillar.

'What vexes you, O Priest?' the Astrologer asked.

'We have failed,' the Priest said. 'Failed through sloth. You failed to pierce the foetal umbrella and I failed to pierce the goddess's silence.'

'Yes,' the Astrologer said. 'We did not pray enough.'

The Priest threw open the begrimed doors of the sanctum, the cymbals clanged and bells chimed and incense rose like the breath of stone. He bowed, then prostrated, and against the goddess's pedestal bruised his forehead in the pain of the peasants. After this frenzy of worship, he turned to the Astrologer, 'Now we begin reading.'

'Yes,' the Astrologer said.

'We read till sunset, we read into the night, and the next morning. Will you, brother, join me on this voyage?'

With a bow the Astrologer sat down to the litany.

*

In the small hours of the morning they heard the sound of wailing from the village.

'This is no ordinary cry,' the Astrologer said. 'Let us go and see for ourselves.' The Priest and the Astrologer rose. As the Priest was about to place the book of litany back in the locker, the Astrologer barred him, 'Take it with you, O Priest.' They set out to where the cry came from. The Priest led the way, book in hand. In a lane they encountered a scion of the gentry, wide-eyed and frenzied. 'Sir,' the Priest asked, 'what means the cry?'

'Punishment, the Law,' the scion answered. 'A peasant couple tried to flee the village, but the Sovereign intercepted them.' Having said this, he raised a slogan to the Sovereign and ran away down the lane. The Priest and the Astrologer quickened their pace.

There was no crowd before the peasant couple's hut. The wail came from the neighbours who stood outside their own homesteads and watched the hut. The hut itself was guarded by a ring of little foetuses, the flicker of oil lamps a lurid orange on their armours of membrane. The foetuses heaved themselves up, their hands raised; the Priest held the book high and strode up to them undeterred, and the phalanx parted. Vessels and bundles of clothing, the peasants' possessions, lay scattered in the yard. The Priest and the Astrologer entered the hut. There, on the narrow verandah, the couple lay dead, the sign of the red abrasion on their necks. Their little son sat beside them and cried. And on the corpse of the woman, naked and bleeding between the thighs, perched the punishing Foetus.

The book in the Priest's hands now moved with a subtle oscillation of power. He pressed it to his bosom, and the Force, like a hundred needles of ecstasy, permeated his body. 'Touch me, O Astrologer,' the Priest said. The Astrologer laid a hand on the Priest's shoulder, and the Force surged into him. '*Devee*, goddess!' the Priest called out to the temple far away. The Foetus shifted around on the corpse like a trapped squid, and lifted its eyes—rheumy carbuncles— towards the book.

'O Incarnation,' the Priest spoke with power, 'is this just?'

The Foetus winced. From the slit that was its mouth issued forth indistinct metallic curses. The Priest went on, 'No, Unborn Thing! This is not just.' And to the Astrologer he said, 'Brother, let us sit down and read the litany.'

They sat down beside the corpses, and oblivious to the encircling horror, began chanting. Impassioned and musical, the verses rose to the brooding canopy of death and bounced back on the Foetus in a shower of subtle droplets, a rain of love. On the slimy hide love turned to pain. Pausing in the litany, the Priest now spoke to the Foetus, not in power but in tenderness, 'O Unborn Child, look at your little brother whom you have orphaned. The redemption for your curse lies not in the sorrow of others.'

They resumed the litany. Presently they heard the metallic voice rise to a sharp and different pitch. The Foetus was crying! Suddenly, slithering down from the corpse, it moved towards the child and paused before his crossed legs. Then it reached out and began to caress the boy and anoint him with penitent slime.

'Goddess, Mother!' the Priest cried in joyous invocation. Then as they listened incredulously, a weird echo came from the Foetus, 'Goddess, Mother!'

Overcoming his revulsion and nausea, the Priest leaned forward and laid his hand on the Foetus's forehead in benediction. 'Return, son,' he said, 'to your mother's womb, and be born as a child.'

The hut was filled with the Foetus's weeping, the weeping spilled to the yard. The Foetus ploughed through this sorrow and slithered out, down the steps, across the yard and past the gate. The Priest and the Astrologer were met outside by a willless ring of little weeping foetuses. Dotting the yard were the scions of the gentry, deeply adream in foetal crouch. The Foetus was now painfully moving down the lane. The Priest and the Astrologer followed it with gentle attention. The Priest handed the book to the Astrologer, and stooping over the Foetus, said, 'Son, you are not a leader but an embryo. The gravel on the lane will hurt your tender skin. I shall carry you.'

The Foetus let itself be carried, unresisting, like the unborn infant it was. Nestling in the arms of the Priest it wept again. The three of them made their journey thus to the fortress. At the fortress's gate, the Priest put down the Foetus, and said, 'May the goddess forgive us all!'

On the seventh day, black clouds gathered over the fortress and bolts of lightning crashed on the bronze domes. The arching banyans, primordial spiders, caught fire with an agonized whistling. The dogs howled to their deaths and great bats winged out of the fortress into the raging fire. A solitary chamber-maid, beating her breast and wailing, emerged from the fortress wading through its doom with a message for the village.

*

'The news is grim,' the Priest spoke to the Astrologer in the temple, 'The Lady delivered. The child was still-born and the mother too passed away.'

They walked to the village. In the lanes and on the common and beside the stiles sat the scions of the gentry, despairing, wailing, freed into insanity. The little foetuses lay scattered, dead and rotting.

'Enough,' the Priest said. 'Let us return to the temple.'

A new peace filled the deserted temple, the grace of the awakened goddess. The Priest and the Astrologer sat down on the verandah. 'Now ask the planets, O Astrologer.'

'I shall.'

The Astrologer cast his shells. There was a smile on his face.

'The planets are no longer hidden for us. The foetal eclipse has passed.'

There was hope and redemption in the cowrie shells. They revealed the refulgent signs of the stars, the chart of freedom!

Oil

The sun shone over the scrub and the wind blew free. The spaces of the sun and the wind were infinite, they stretched from the scrub to the mountain peaks and the tides of the sea. Nothing touched the tedious tangle of the scrub, neither the light nor the movement, yet the scrub blossomed at far intervals, its flowers like inward eyes of endurance and quiet hope. The sun sank and the wind grew cold; another day had ended in the village...

The share-cropper Pazhanimala came to Ayyan Chettiyar's shop with some trepidation, for he had come to borrow money and custom forbade such transaction after the lamps were lit. But Ayyan Chettiyar put the share-cropper at ease, 'There's always an emergency. What do you need it for?' Such was Ayyan Chettiyar's kindness.

'My boy has taken ill,' Pazhanimala said. 'Looks like rheumatism.'

'Merciful gods!' the Chettiyar said, handing the share-cropper five rupees. 'Your child is fifteen if I remember it right. Is that an age for rheumatism?'

'That's what bothers me.'

Rheumatoid illnesses rarely afflict the young, yet the child had all the symptoms of such a seizure, hands and legs grown limp. It had been so for seven days, and home-made unctions and warm poultices had done nothing to relieve the affliction.

'O Chalachi,' the Chettiyar called out to his wife in the back of the shop which was their house, 'did you hear this? Our Pazhanimala's boy has rheumatism.'

Chalachi Chettichiyar peeped out, 'Rheumatism, did you say?'

'Looks like it,' Pazhanimala said.

'Merciful gods!' the Chettichiyar said. 'I shall come and have a look in a little while.'

As Pazhanimala walked home with the money, he thought again of the Chettiyar's generosity and concern. Of the three hundred villagers, the majority were share-croppers and farm-hands. They had no rights over their lands or work; the land-lords who lived outside the village—men of unapproachable upper castes—often imposed a burdensome indebtedness on them. But invariably the Chettiyar came to their rescue with money and with household needs on credit.

Unlike other money-lenders, the Chettiyar charged but a reasonable interest, and his weights and measures could be trusted. He would wait from sowing to harvest to get his money back, and for this the peasant women were grateful, but they were even more grateful to the Chettichiyar who ministered to their private illnesses with herbal specifics. The one most in use was a brew of banyan root, a cure for menstrual disorders, and there was practically no woman in the village who had not benefited from this remedy at one time or the other. It was more than just medicine because the Chettichiyar stripped the women and felt their soft privacies. Then she told her husband of her discoveries before coming back to the women; it was an erotic compact of sorts. The Chettiyars were immigrants, oil millers from across the mountain pass. The Chettiyar's father had hawked oil in the village, but, by the time the Chettiyar was grown up, there was enough money to set up a primitive oil press and a little shop which sold not only oil but sundry kitchen things as well. The press was turned by an aged and diminutive bull which walked round and round with a benign expression on its face. The father, the hawker was dead, and the son, after he had acquired the press and the shop, fetched for himself a bride from across the mountain pass, the Chettichiyar. She became the most impressive woman in the village, of a statuesque alien breed. She took elaborate baths in the village tank, smearing the paste of turmeric on her cheeks, and oil on her large black breasts. In good time she had a daughter, who grew up as statuesque and alien as her mother; she, in turn, stood on the waterfront smearing turmeric and oil…

The Chettichiyar visited the ailing child late that night. The child lay on a bed of straw, covered by shreds of blanket and gunny bags. She prescribed medicines, root essences and oils, but though the ministration went on for days, the paralysis got worse.

A barefoot village officer, who made his rounds between two small towns, often visited the village. During one of his visits, he was told about the child's disease. He examined the child, and said that perhaps it wasn't rheumatism after all, that it might be dangerous to treat the disease on such an assumption, and that it might be better to take the child to Palghat, the town six miles away, to be shown to the English medicine man. This was not enough to shake the share-cropper's trust in the Chettichiyar's remedies; he persisted in the oils and potions. The paralysis grew, and in another week the child was dead. The Chettiyar and the Chettichiyar consoled the share-cropper. Pazhanimala had lost his other child earlier, and his land tenure after the last harvest, and had no real right to his homestead. Thus bereaved and ruined he took the emigrant's track out of the village.

A few days later a farm-hand who had come to get his groceries informed Ayyan Chettiyar, 'Our hunchback is down with fever.'

The Chettiyar smothered a smile of amusement beneath his enormous moustache, and said, 'I suppose his woman is on a visit to the village.'

'I suppose so,' the farm-hand said.

'What damnation!' the Chettiyar said, and then called out to his wife, 'Hear this, O Chalachi? The hunchback's woman is back and so is his fever.' In the living quarters behind the shop, Chalachi Chettichiyar and her grown-up daughter giggled.

The hunchback did no work in particular; although the Chettiyar maintained him with generous doles, he was no mere dependant. He lazed about the village and occasionally hobbled to town and watched the trading with lewd disinterest. It was some years ago that his wife had eloped with a Muslim cart driver and moved to the town where she had become a Muslim, even dressing as one, with the large scarf over her hair, the deep bordered sarong and silver girdle. All the years she had spent in the hunchback's bed she had menstruated in desperation, and now, as the jibe went in the village, delivered at the mere sight of her handsome cartman.

She produced a brood of robust children in quick succession, and her breasts were never dry. She made frequent visits to the village, the scene of her former chastity, with her daughters in tow, their numerous silver anklets jingling noisily. During each of these visits she would parade herself in front of her old house, her plentiful udders covered by daring skintight tops. Then the fever would come over the hunchback, and he would take to bed for days on end. Slowly recovering, he would go drunk to the Chettiyar's shop to listen to his mentor's words of consolation.

This time the Chettiyar told his wife, 'Go and tend to him. Also find out if he has brought the oil.'

Well after dusk, with her daughter in attendance, the Chettichiyar went to the hunchback's house. In a room that was like a garbage bin, the hunchback lay knotted in his bed.

'O hunchback,' the Chettichiyar called out, 'look up.'

He opened his eyes, and lay still without undoing the knots of his misshapen body.

'What is the matter with you?' the Chettichiyar asked. 'The fever again?'

'Mmmm,' the hunchback replied wretchedly.

The Chettichiyar went over and sat on his bed. Closing the door from the inside, the daughter leaned against it.

'Have you brought the oil from the town?' the Chettichiyar enquired.

'Mmmm.'

'Is that whore on a visit here again?'

The question brought tears to his eyes, and he was seized with a spasm of crying. The daughter leaning against the door giggled.

'Hunchback,' the Chettichiyar said, 'why do you cry, just because she is stomping about in the village?'

She felt his forehead, and true enough it was fevered.

'Take heart,' she said. 'I shall put a wet compress on your forehead.'

Chalachi Chettichiyar pulled a pouch off her waist, and from it took out a smattering of medicament which she crushed into fine powder in a bronze ladle. Then she displaced her saree from her shoulder and undid the buttons of her jacket. The hunchback watched in dismay as her large-teated breasts spilled out; the daughter leaning against the door giggled. The Chettichiyar began a stream of gossip, stroking her breasts the while and squirting milk into the ladle.

'Lie still, O hunchback,' she said. 'I am getting your compress ready.' She worked the breastmilk and medicament into a thick slush, and her breasts looming over the hunchback, the dark discs round their teats like shields of battle, spread it over the fevered forehead. Then pulling out her hairpins and holding them between her lips, she began teasing her hair into an elaborate coiffure. The sick man lay watching her, his eyes mesmerized by her gently heaving breasts.

'Where is the oil?' the Chettichiyar asked between the seductive movements of her hair.

'In the kitchen,' the hunchback answered feebly.

'How much?'

'Eight measures.'

The Chettichiyar shoved her breasts under cover, and rose and went into the kitchen. There in a corrugated drum was the oil the hunchback had brought from town. Carrying the drum on her head she walked back home. Ayyan Chettiyar was waiting.

'How much?' the Chettiyar asked.

'Eight measures,' she replied.

'How is his fever?'

'I have put a compress.'

As the Chettichiyar was heaving the drum of oil into the living quarters, Velunni, another share-cropper, came to the shop.

'O Chettichiyar,' he said, 'please come home with me. My son has taken ill.' Rajan, the boy, was just fifteen, and yet he was seized with the same rheumatoid sickness that had killed Pazhanimala's son.

A week later, two more children were afflicted, and Rajan, meanwhile, was paralyzed up to the waist. Chalachi Chettichiyar visited the sick children. The disease seemed to be spreading; no one till then had known paralysis as a contagion. The village elders conferred, and one of them suggested that there might be some contamination in the water. They poured purifying herbal potions into their wells, smeared the Chettichiyar's medicated oils on their children's limbs, and tried to revive them with hot poultices. The Chettichiyar made cold compresses with the breastmilk of other women, stripping them for the purpose and ritually fondling their teats. The spreading paralysis showed no signs of abating.

Several days after the children had fallen ill, the village officer passed that way again. 'God!' he said, when he knew of the number of children affected — as many as thirty. For some strange reason the older people and the very young were immune; the paralysis struck only the pubescent children. Although thus far there had been only one fatality—Pazhanimala's child—the officer decided the strange epidemic was a serious matter. He resolved to stay in the village for a day and investigate. As he went around questioning the parents of the sick children, he came by certain coincidences. The spade-man, Kuttiappu, and the loader Rami, lived in adjacent huts, and their children were struck down at the same time. Sitting cross-legged on the floor of Kuttiappu's hut he began with great patience to question his wife. 'Try to remember,' he said, 'whether you ate anything unusual these last few days?'

Kuttiappu was away in the fields; Kuttiappu's woman was doubly reticent because she was alone and the questioner was an officer of the government.

'We have broken no law,' she said.

The officer took the proffered betel leaves, symbol of hospitality, he chewed them with relish and began gossiping about the village and the town playing for her confidence. It was then that he noticed that she was constantly untangling her hair, with a repetitiveness that seemed unnatural, as though some invisible adhesive was matting the freed strands of her hair again and again. He asked, 'What's the matter with your hair?'

'That is what I'm wondering too,' she said, embarrassed at his intimate observation. 'The other day I had an oil bath, and ever since then the hair feels funny.'

'When did you bathe last?'

'I can't recollect, some days ago.'

'How often do you bathe?'

'Once a month.'

That was the purification bath; she was reminded of her periods, and grew shy. Giving her time to recover, the officer continued, 'Which means that the strange feeling in the hair has something to do with the oil.'

She answered with an indecisive sibilant. The officer pursued his logic, 'So obviously, it's the oil.'

Kuttiappu's woman was stumped for an answer. Her eyes downcast, she worked her fingers nervously through the invisible adhesive. But the officer's mind was elsewhere: he was thinking of oil, only of oil, with frenzied concentration. He asked, 'Did you season your curries with the same oil?'

'We eat food unseasoned. Can't afford the seasoning.'

'But once in a while?'

'Wait a minute!' she said, recollecting. 'We did fry *vellappams*.'

'When was that?'

She hesitated, as though a mysterious injunction was stopping her.

The village officer left her and walked up to the hut of Kuppayi-achchan, the village elder. 'Elder,' he said, 'it just struck me. Could the oil possibly be adulterated?'

The elder was unwilling even to speculate upon the possibility; gratitude forbade it. It was the Chettiyar who sold them the oil they needed for the monthly baths, and for the occasional frying of *vellappams*. His weights and measures were scrupulously honest and he sold groceries on easy credit. The Chettiyar's family had done so for two generations. The elder pleaded with the officer, 'Please, please leave the Chettiyar out of this. God bless him.'

'I was not insinuating,' the officer said, hastily retreating. 'Still it will hurt no one to get the oil analyzed.'

The officer visited the rheumatoid houses one by one. In each of them women, their tresses down, were battling with the unseen adhesive. And in each of them, patient questioning revealed, they had fried *vellappams*. At sundown he decided to go to the Chettiyar's shop.

'You crush all this oil yourself?' he asked the Chettiyar.

The Chettiyar smiled, the smile spread beneath his mesh of moustache and was hidden eerily, 'Sit down, Sir. You must be tired from the journey.'

'Tired, yes,' the officer replied sitting down. 'It's a long way to cycle.'

'I 'm honoured by this visit.'

'I came to do a little shopping,' the officer said, chewing the betel offered him. 'Give me a rupee's worth of oil.'

The Chettiyar craned his neck and called out to the living quarters at the back of the shop, 'O Chalachi, fetch some oil for our officer here. Pour out a large measure.'

The Chettiyar made no attempt to dip into the drums kept in the shop itself. The oil was to be taken from the stores inside.

'I don't need a large measure,' the officer said. 'Just a rupee's worth.' And he pointed to the oil drums on display. 'From these.'

The Chettiyar's smile spread wider, and the mesh expanded to absorb it. Chalachi Chettichiyar also came to the doorway, and stood there making her sumptuous presence felt.

'I've some very special oil inside,' the Chettiyar said, 'the best sun-dried coconut I have ever crushed. You have honoured me by this visit, I need to give you something special.'

'Oh, that's kind of you, but the oil in this drum here will do.'

'O Chalachi, make it a measure-and-a-half of our special oil. This is our officer come from town, come pedalling all the way. It is an honour. And don't take any money from him.'

The Chettichiyar withdrew for a moment, to reappear with a canister. This time the officer stopped her a little sternly, 'Not that oil, but this, from this drum.'

The smile froze and vanished behind the mesh; the Chettiyar said, 'You're our officer after all, and I might as well tell you the truth. A little castor oil got mixed up with this stock, and you know how castor leaves a bad taste. It was a slip. Chalachi here forgets to clean the drums.'

He was getting somewhere now, the officer thought. Ayyan Chettiyar had admitted the oil was contaminated, however inadvertently. If it was castor, one could taste the oil and find out. The officer stretched his hand towards the drum to dip a finger. The next instant Chalachi Chettichiyar had barred him, her supple hand on his. The Chettiyar had regained his composure and said, 'Let him.' Chalachi Chettichiyar eased her grip but still her palm, soft and sensuous, lay on the officer, and he had the curious feeling that it was secretly gliding back and forth over his wrist. She smelt sensuous, the smell of oil enhancing her body's pungence; he felt subtly deterred.

He left the village without dipping his finger into the drum and finding out if the oil was adulterated with castor. The little township of Kottekad, where he stayed, was some seven miles away. He had barely pedalled half the distance, when suddenly an enormous bundle of bamboo thorns stood up in front of him on the unlit path and began crazily to rotate. He had heard of sorcerers who could animate bundles of thorn and set them on people; a chill crept over his hands and legs, his grip loosened on the handlebars, and he fell unconscious. When he came to himself it was the last *yaama*, a mystic measure of the night; the constellation of the seven sages was dipping westward. In the moonless sky, the stars shone with strange plumes of light. He rose with great effort, almost blacking out as he took a few unsteady steps along the mud track. Giving up, he sat down beside his fallen bicycle; just then a great beetle appeared, flew around him thrice with the tumult of a mountain stream, and disappeared into the night. Certainly a sorcerer's familiar. When the beetle was gone, the officer pressed his palm deep into the cold dust and the touch of earth revived him.

When he reached home, he lay in a fever for days. 'For my sake,' his wife said, 'keep away from that accursed village.' She had heard about Ayyan Chettiyar's sorcery, that he communed with poltergeists. He recalled the bamboo thorns and the beetle like a muted nightmare. Though he feebly contemplated resuming the investigation the prolonged fever had broken his will, he gave up in the end. The nightmare faded altogether after that and he wondered how he had ever strayed into its grimy labyrinths. One little memory was to return though, the caressing palm, obscenely traversing his wrist, but its very guilt scared him away from confronting it again.

*

Rajan's hands and legs had begun shrivelling, his fingers stiffening into brittle twigs. His face alone shone with a defiant light. Two of his class-fellows came to visit him. They found him lying on a narrow strip of verandah, watching the sun go down. He lay thinking of the days before the illness crippled him, when he used to trek the seven miles to school enjoying the wooded country-side that lay about him. His father was away in the fields, and his mother gathered firewood in the scrub.

'You are alone, Rajan?' enquired Narayanan and Govindan in concern.

The lonely boy smiled; he was the handsomest among his class-fellows, but today his shrivelling limbs filled Narayanan and Govindan with grief and loathing. They slipped under his cot a satchelful of oranges, the gift villagers carry while visiting the sick. They sat down beside him and talked. Rajan was eager for school gossip. A girl in the tenth standard, his friends told him, was in love with the Sanskrit instructor; a black monkey invaded the classroom at lunch break; and their football team had qualified for the finals next week. Rajan had been the school's star footballer, the team's aggressive forward. He listened, his feeble legs once again remembering the joy of the fast passes; the exuberance of the tournament sprung before him only to quieten down as sunset images.

'Our School Day comes next month,' Govindan said. 'Get well by then.'

Rajan answered sadly, 'No, Govindan. It does not look like I will get well.'

They did not speak much thereafter. The friends rose to go.

'Govindan...' began Rajan, lingering over the farewell. He wanted to tell them what he had overheard, the words of the village officer, who had told his father that there might be a lethal adulterant in the Chettiyar's oil. It was in great detail that the officer had talked about the *vellappams* and the women's matted hair. But, since then, neither his father nor his mother had spoken of it again. Rajan spent his lonely evenings recalling the words of the officer, and the Chettiyar and his wife, and the oil press and the sick old bull which worked the press treading round and round, grew within him into a lurid nightmare, a nightmare which lay on his generation like a curse. The sadness of the parting prevailed over his fear, and Rajan said, 'Narayanan, it's the oil. The oil is poisoned, it has brought on the sickness. It is no use telling anyone in this village. Tell your father, Narayanan, tell him to go to the police for us. Tell him, won't you?'

Tears fell from Rajan's eyes...Govindan and Narayanan began their journey back to their own village. It was from Ayyan Chettiyar's shop that they picked up the torches of palm fibre which would light their way. The nightmare had subtly sunk into their minds as well, and as they collected their change from the Chettiyar their gaze rested briefly on his face, on the forbidding mesh of moustache, on the eyes evil and yellowing and on the tuft of hair tied in a grotesque knot. Behind him stood his daughter, nubile and luscious, ogling greedily at them. The tableau was both luring and oppressive, and as they walked back along the mud track, waving their torches to make them light up in the wind, the fear grew within them even more.

The visit of Govindan and Narayanan was their last ever, they kept away from the village. Rajan pleaded with Velunni, 'Father, will you send for Govindan or Narayanan?' Velunni merely fell silent, and sat looking at his crippled son; in helpless persistence Rajan tried to reach him past the stupor, 'Father...' The cry did not reach Velunni, the stupor had dulled his ears, and let his eyes wander far away. He rose and waddled out of the house.

*

For some days now Rajan had been repeatedly pleading with his father to take the oil to where they could identify the mix, to the laboratory in the city beyond the mountain pass. On each of those occasions Velunni's reason would revive briefly, and he would fantasize a journey to the city. He would rehearse it futilely only to retreat into the stupor each time...

Velunni stepped out of his gate and made for the village common. The sunset was turning to cold dusk.

'Velunni-etta! Velunni-etta!' the hunchback accosted him on the way. 'Where are you going?'

'Nowhere in particular.'

'How is the boy?'

Velunni did not reply but walked on. The hunchback hobbled alongside.

'Velunni-etta,' the hunchback said, 'when that village officer was here, did you talk to him?'

Velunni hedged.

'Come clean,' the hunchback insisted.

'I'm sorry, I did talk.'

'How could you, Velunni-etta? How could you do a thing like that?'

Velunni did not know where he was going, he walked with the hunchback, as if drawn by an invisible current in a river. Presently they entered a lane with tall embankments on either side, a footpath cut deep into the earth. On the embankments grew ancient bamboo, tangled with thorns and the interminable lace of spiders' webs. It was just dusk but the lane was sunk in the gloom of bamboo thickets. As they walked deeper into the footpath the mystic darkness grew ink-black.

'You ought not to have done it,' Velunni heard the hunchback's admonition. A shivering seized Velunni, a thousand lancets of fear. The lane choked with its darkness, its time frozen and alien. He saw that the gentle glow of dusk still lit the huts that lay beyond the thickets. But these human habitations seemed to be an incredible distance away. A mute cry rose within him to the fathers and mothers of crippled children, it died down like a serpent swaying itself to death. Could he cry again, could he pierce this darkness with the cry? Velunni gave up, because he knew that in the huts beyond the bamboo they would fortify their ears against this call of doom. Each of them existed in his or her own separate darkness, on the darkness's sufferance, each under the oppression of his or her own personal hunchback.

After what seemed like an age of incarceration, Velunni emerged from the lane. Outside, on the pasture, there was the lucid glow of sunset, but still the fear clung to him like a giant leech. The hunchback had gone his way, and Velunni, circling the pasture, got back to the grounds outside his gate, where, leaning on a guava tree, he watched his son asleep on the verandah. A little lamp lit Rajan's face like an icon of suffering.

*

It was four years ago that the disease had first struck the village, today its entire youth was a crippled generation. The younger ones grew up in health till pubescence, only to be claimed by the great paralysis. The children lay, one vast scrub of twig-like limbs, and the elders, their reason blighted, wandered distraught through the scrub…

Chalachi Chettichiyar had concocted a new herbal ointment. Ayyan Chettiyar recommended this to the village, to the young and old alike, to the crippled ones as to those unaffected. The hunchback made his pre-dawn knocks and threatened those who had neglected the injunction, and monitored the progress of those who had smeared on the medicament.

'Don't you feel good?' he would ask them.

'We can't say yet,' some of the parents would reply.

'Tsk! Tsk!' the hunchback would say. 'How will any medicine take effect if you are so half-hearted and sceptical? You need faith.'

'True,' they would assent weakly. 'We need faith.'

Along with the ointment, the Chettiyar laid down prescriptions of diet, and recommended continence and temperance. The Chettichiyar surprised the women, and invaded their privacies for evidence of indulgence. And the hunchback lay crouching in the dark on the outskirts of the village to catch hold of the delinquent men returning from the tavern in the next village. He led them into the presence of the Chettiyar.

'What have you done, my little brothers?' the Chettiyar would chastize them severely yet with compassion.

'It was a mistake, Chettiyar.'

The Chettichiyar would join in the disapprobation. 'Of what use is it to merely own up to the mistake?'

'Forgive us, kind ones!'

As their children lay paralyzed, what made them sneak out in the dark to the tavern, their unlit treks crossing the deadly serpent trails? Such thirst was calamitous defiance; beneath the placid layers of the mind, secret powers thirsted for defiance. Had these men realized the meaning of the thirst they would have given way and disintegrated; now in their protective ignorance, they stood before the Chettiyar, delinquent cretins, and let the drawling monotone of reproach fall on them like the drops of water from a torturer's spigot. When they confessed to their sin, and gave themselves up to the wisdom of punishment, the monotone transmuted itself into consolation.

Neighbouring villages heard of the paralysis, and guessed much more. None of them wanted to get involved with the tragic destiny of another community, they only took care not to let the Chettiyar's oil into their own shops. This hurt the Chettiyar a little, but his profits fell in no significant measure, because all the three hundred families in the village bought more and more of his oil, and when the illness and the consequent distraction and incapacity brought on debts, the Chettiyar quietly annexed their tiny strips of land. But they stayed on in the village, landless, their homesteads held on sufferance; they lost the will to seek work elsewhere, to cross the boundaries of the village for the strange breath of freedom. As the days went by, they forgot the taste of freshly pressed oil; the grimy dog-eared ledger in which was chronicled their debt, the Chettiyar with his hypnotic mask, the Chettichiyar with her wild teats, the hunchback, hobbling and persecuting, the endless scrub of shrivelled limbs, this became their environment. Only the hunchback travelled out of the village every Saturday; he went to town and from one of its dismal alleys bought a colourless fluid, dense as grease, an inexpensive chemical waste. He brought it back to the village where the Chettiyar and the Chettichiyar processed it and mixed it in edible oil. It had taken them some time to arrive at the right mix, just short of the fatal. It was when they had bid for too much profit that share-cropper Pazhanimala's son had died. From now on no one would die, they would only be paralyzed.

*

A whole generation lay with limbs lost to movement and sentience. The next generation waited for the paralysis.

Velunni's Rajan was going to be twenty. One day Ayyan Chettiyar sent for Velunni. When Velunni arrived at the shop the Chettiyar was tightening the screws of a new device. It was a machine that would press the oil from now on. The old bullock-driven press lay uprooted.

'The bull cannot do it anymore,' the Chettiyar said. 'It's ill.'

For years the bullock, yoked to the oil press, had plodded along a changeless circle, crushing seed and coconut into oil for its master. But now the years of the draught animal had ended, and its pacific presence was replaced by the tireless and inexorable machine, the village's new malefic god. Gone were the memories of the Chettiyar's father as itinerant hawker, who visited the huts, a smile beneath his mesh, selling the pure extract of seed and coconut. In their place now was a new and subtle mastery.

'Little brother,' the Chettiyar said, 'we gather that your son is turning twenty.'

'It is so, O Chettiyar.'

The Chettiyar motioned to Velunni to sit beside him, a gesture of concern and respect. They shared the leaf of the betel vine.

'I've given it a great deal of thought,' the Chettiyar said. 'It's time we chose a bride for the boy. I think Janu, daughter of Rakkanagan, will make a good wife. *She's seventeen. I want this marriage before the next harvest.*'

The words flowed smoothly out of the mesh, words of insistent power. A bride for his crippled son was a precious evasive fear, and now Velunni, left with no exit, confronted the awful reality, a crippled bride. A wedding without hands and legs, the promise of limbless progeny.

Reason floundered and turned away from the terror, seeking the sanctuary of compliance. *All thinking is horrendous, so I shall not think, Velunni said to himself, think for me, O Compassionate One, and beam reassurance from behind your hieratic mesh.*

*

The marriage was celebrated in the Chettiyar's benign presence, the village's first ever solemnization of torsos. The guests trooped in cheerlessly, and partook of boiled rice and sweetened pulses, and without lingering dispersed into the night. When the last of them had left, Velunni and his wife carried the inert bride to where the boy lay. For one brief moment father and son looked into each other's eyes.

'Father, why did you do this?'

Velunni turned away, but Rajan raised his voice after him, 'Has this bloody offering appeased the Chettiyar?'

Something churned within Velunni, a sad and venomous froth, it spiralled up and blotted out his hearing. Rajan spoke on, 'Father, have you gone to the Chettiyar's house and enquired after the health of his children? None of them has got this sickness.'

Velunni pressed his palms to his forehead in despair and penitence. 'My son, you sin with these words,' he said.

'Let me sin, my father. Look at my hands and legs, what more punishment can there be and for what sin?'

Velunni's wife beat her breast. 'O my son,' she wailed, 'how can you speak like this to your father?'

The talking and the wailing stopped abruptly; they had seen the slouched figure cross the gate and hobble across the yard. The hunchback entered the hut and sat cross-legged on the low rise of the plinth.

'What was the talk about?' he asked.

Rajan forced a smile and said, 'Aw, we were just talking away.'

'I heard,' the hunchback said. 'I heard it all.'

Velunni and his wife stood suppliant with palms joined before the nocturnal listener. 'Children talk without wisdom,' Velunni said. 'Do not burden your mind with it.'

'My mind? Forget about my mind, but think of how hurt the Chettiyar will be when he comes to know.'

The silence was tangible, an incubus. Then Rajan spoke with the frenzied belligerence of the torso, 'Yes, let the Chettiyar know. He ought to.'

Velunni and his woman, and even Rajan himself, froze as the words were spoken. The hunchback rose, and weirdly pirouetting, began kicking the boy. He kicked the bony chest, and stamped on the stems of hands and legs in a weak fury, falling back with the effort of each charge only to return to the attack in a torrent of abuse like the sorcerer's beetle. His fury spent, the hunchback hobbled down from the plinth to the yard, 'The Chettiyar feeds, the Chettiyar medicates, the Chettiyar finds you mates. He does everything and, yet—ungrateful dogs!'

The hunchback left, the silence extended like a contagion, from hut to hut, stilling the landscape of the night. From these perilous refuges, men listened without sympathy.

The night had gone far. In the little room which was theirs Rajan and Janu brought their limbless bodies close.

'Did it hurt?' Janu asked, with sudden wifely maturity. Rajan smiled.

'No.'

'Henceforth we shall not talk of the Chettiyar. Nor think of him.'

'We shall not.'

'You have me.' Janu said. 'To talk to and think of.'

You're mine, Rajan spoke within himself, *I have you, only you.* In that knowing, all else withered away as unreal: the face of the Chettiyar, inscrutable and menacing, the mutant, hobbling in the night and crouching behind thickets to catch the whispered heresies about the oil. A breeze blew outside, and Janu raised her face and flared her nostrils. Rajan sensed her discomfort.

'What is it Janu?'

'There's a smell in the air. It's evil.'

True, the smell; it came in the wind, along chartless trails, rising and falling in gentle spasms like the pain of a growing tumour.

'Oh that?' Rajan said. 'The old bull of the oil press died. The hunchback and the outcastes hauled its carcass to the burial ground. They have left it there to rot.'

'The poor dear,' Janu said.

Both of them remembered their childhood and the years of the pious animal. Playing about near the oil press, excited by its trundling, its slow certainty, the children would count each rotation. They fancied the bull acknowledged their counting and nodded at them. They fancied it smiled. All its life it had followed its sad orbit, pressing the Chettiyar's oil, and now, its orbit ended, it rode the wind of the mountain pass.

'Janu...'

Rajan saw tears in her eyes. Her lips were red, the red of the flower in the scrub. He breathed in those lips as he would the flower's fragrance.

*

Two days later an agent of the District Board and a barefoot officer of the Health Department came to the Chettiyar's shop and demanded a specimen of the oil for examination. The news spread through the village. It was rumoured that a complaint had been lodged by the hunchback's former wife, the one who had run away with the cartman to feed and multiply. For the first time in years a desire to know gripped the village, the scrub burst into sudden bloom. Then, as suddenly as they had come, the flowers withered, and the knowing gave way to cheerless prudence. The villagers saw the officers sitting in the Chettiyar's shop drinking potent country liquor. The sounds of the carousing mingled with the screams of chickens being slaughtered for the feast.

At night, wined and feasted, the officers and the Chettiyar sat long, chewing betel. Close to midnight they retired to the annexe the Chettiyar had built for guests. Two beds had been made and laid close to each other, and on these the officers lay down. In a little while the Chettichiyar and her daughter came in with cups of milk for the guests. The night was cooling down and when the wind rose the man from the Health Department asked the daughter, 'What's that smell?' She merely shook her head in the dark. The man from the District Board asked Chalachi Chettichiyar, 'What's that smell?'

Chalachi Chettichiyar unbuttoned her blouse, in the dark her big breasts soft solids of a denser darkness. 'It's the smell of musk,' the Chettichiyar said. The man from the District Board buried his face in the pungent cleft. There indeed was a smell like that of the scented secretion of the civet cat or of rotting chrysanthemums. He sought the variations of the musk in the Chettichiyar's sweating armpits and between her forbidding buttocks. From the mysterious far night rose the dark wind again and swamped the fetid perfume. Although the Chettichiyar snuggled beneath the man from the District Board, festering in her own carnal musk, he flared his nostrils again and took in anxious breaths...

The pious bull, friend of the children, was long gone. Only its carcass lay behind to rot, the body which had plodded round in captive orbit, the length of a wronged lifetime. As its pacific elements disintegrated, the wrong rose from it in spite and violence which the bull itself had not known when it lived. It rose as the avenging stench of death and rode the wind into the village. It raged through the scrub, it tossed its locks in lament for the shrivelled limbs, beat its breast of mist with unseen spectral hands and reared in wrath over the sleep of sinners.

The Examination

As he ascended the final steps Venugopalan's mind was afloat with lightness. It was as though he had sat alone on a riverside, sat the length of a lifetime, and recalled every memory in an act of cleansing; in this recall loomed the events which followed the advent of Ananthan Pillai.

It was in the plague epidemic of 1946 that Ananthan Pillai came to the little backwoods town of Palghat, in whose principal street, where today are situated a money-lender's clandestine bank and a fake apothecary's dispensary, he commandeered a vacant shop and turned it into a plague control outpost. This dingy street was redolent with history, it was called Sultanpet, to commemorate Tippu Sultan's invasion. It was a sad street, its muddy sidewalks full of moisture. One would have thought that it was a strange residue from the rains, but the damp was really the making of aboriginal women. These women, honey-tinted and bare-breasted, cut fodder from the foothills and brought it in headloads to sell to the horse-cartmen in town. With the green loads on their heads, they gossiped, leisurely haggling with their buyers, and enlivened the conversation by making water where they stood. This was easy, since they wore no underclothing. It also gave the buyers an erotic incentive. The piss of numerous evenings mouldered in dark, sad-scented clods. It was in this damp avenue that Ananthan Pillai established himself. Upto that time only ten people had died in Palghat from the epidemic, and the surviving members of the families tended to hush up the nature of the deaths, because it was the bubonic plague, and the carbuncles which appeared on the groin were initially mistaken for the disease of pleasure and shame. It was only when the carbuncles began appearing on the thighs of children that the people became aware of the nature of the scourge. The town's newspaper, a reluctant commentator, wrote, 'Palghat is a famous town, and it gives us great pride to recall that in the good days of old its twenty square miles were an empire of four kingdoms. It is a pity that this fell disease has attacked such a historic town. People thus afflicted will have their daily observances, like spinning, disrupted. They will experience great inconveniences and possibly death...' The old town appeared to be taking the plague in its stride; but when more of its inhabitants died, the teachers of primary schools began campaigning among the people: *the epidemic is spread by rats, so it is the need of the hour to farm cats to control the disease without state intervention.*

Behind the shops of Sultanpet were the tenements of the Chettiyars, an immigrant clan who sported tufts of hair and worshipped Ganapathy, the one-tusked elephant god; the rat was the god's vehicle. On an intersection in the street stood the temple of Ganapathy, and the men of the indigenous castes spread the ethnic calumny that the rats were turning the temple into a citadel. It was difficult to ascertain the extent of the Chettiyars' involvement with Ganapathy's rats, but at least this much was known for certain that through years of worshipping Ganapathy most Chettiyars had abnormally elongated left canines. The priest of the temple, Velayuthan Chettiyar, declared that any assault on the temple by the natives would be resisted by the clan. The death toll was now thirty-seven.

But with the coming of Ananthan Pillai the diverse views of the people regarding the disease became irrelevant, the state had taken over rat and parasite and the carbuncle on the thigh. Soon the municipal inoculatress, Chenthamarakshi, the slim, fair, middle-aged beauty who had provided the town's preventive medicine with erotic relief, was inducted as Ananthan Pillai's help.

The plague control centre was a one room shop, open-fronted, with no privacy, and passersby would gaze, fascinated, at the fair woman and her dark, squat chief. There was nothing to do in the initial days except to sit there waiting for the plague to assume epidemic dimensions; tired of long hours on his reclining chair, Ananthan Pillai would step out, once in a while, into the street. With his Hitlerian moustache atwirl, dark, leathery skin aglow, enormous cheroot dangling from pendulous lips , hooked walking stick swinging, Ananthan Pillai would walk up and down the street in his blazer, shorts and felt hat, attempting to convince himself of his own intimidating presence. While the teachers of the primary school sensed in this presence a historic catastrophe, the common folk were placid, and the aboriginal women, as they stood gazing at this new bridgehead of power, pissed unconcerned as usual.

One day as he sat in the plague centre, Ananthan Pillai noticed two of these women across the street, both pretty, one of them with large sultry breasts; Ananthan Pillai concluded that they were of Australoid origin. They stood with their legs splayed, and their single sheath of sarong parted along the middle. He could see their dark and shapely thighs as he sized them up as an anthropologist and administrator. One was carrying an earthen pot of palm brew on her head, and the other a bundle of green fodder. Ananthan Pillai had no objection to people imbibing the brew, as long as it was within limits. His attention turned next to the bundle of fodder, in which, with his expert eye, he identified precious herbs even from a distance. Horses fed on such herbs would haul more and gallop faster, and cows so fed would yield milk in plenty. From the milk his mind wandered to udders, and then to the aboriginal teats, and Ananthan Pillai was satisfied that they were good enough to suckle generations of healthy farm-hands. The country needed such teats, it would be a fitting tribute to the Sovereign. As he watched them, his mind full of nation building, he suddenly saw the earth around their feet getting sodden, then turning to slush. Ananthan Pillai leapt out of his chair. The women did not move even when he positioned himself in front of them. Through the slit in their sarongs two crystalline threads of piss hit the clods and spun round, refracting the sunlight; the women turned a bovine gaze on the officer in their gentle carnal excretion. Suddenly Ananthan Pillai began belabouring them with his hooked walking stick. The women screamed and fled, dropping both palm brew and fodder. Stray donkeys ate up the fodder, while the sweet-sour brew mixed with the piss and settled into the melancholy flavouring of mud.

*

In Venugopalan's house, when told of the beating, grandmother said, 'This does not augur well.' But the grandchildren were excited by the display of sovereign power. They were even more excited when the next day the first two plague policemen appeared outside the plague shop.

The plague policemen wore *khaki* fatigues and red berets, and only those tutored in police lore could read the subtle signs which distinguished them from real policemen. Three more joined them the day after, and by the weekend a detail of twenty plague policemen were lined up along the shop front; behind them Ananthan Pillai rasped *left, right, left, right*. After this brief ceremonial, they broke loose into the side alleys, like the Sultan's hordes who had taken the town a century ago. But the people of Palghat, used as they were to invasions, were not unduly perturbed. They guessed that this new invasion would be directed against the rats, and, at worst, the carbuncled dead who would be grabbed for special disposal.

But this complacency lasted only until the next major incident, which was when Ananthan Pillai walked up to the provisions shop of Muthalif, the aged Muslim trader, and read out a proclamation in the name of the King-Emperor. It was a command to open up the shop for fumigation and lay the hoarded stocks out in the sun to dry. Muthalif was the town's richest man, and no agent of the state had dared to meddle with him until then, because on his wall hung a printed acknowledgement from the the Sultan of Turkey, an impersonal ornate reply to Muthalif's birthday felicitation. It was also rumoured that Muthalif could walk any time into the parlour of Sir Mohammad Usman, the Viceroy's Councillor. The townsfolk knew very little about the Muslim Knight but guessed he held a position equal to that of Sir C. Shankaran Nair, the legendary Hindu judge; such was the respect in which Muthalif was held. Muthalif had no time for minions, and he blithely ignored the Emperor's proclamation, as did his shop assistants, who were busy packaging provisions for customers. Ananthan Pillai waited a minute, and then snared the old man's neck in the crook of his stick, and with one tug brought him tumbling down. Muthalif's handymen cried out in panic. The plague policemen now entered the shop, and assisted by saturnine scavengers, carters of shit, began flinging out the hoarded provisions. With the provisions came a teeming horde of rats and bandicoots. Catching hold of the old man's wispy beard, Ananthan Pillai addressed the awed onlookers, 'Look you, all of you, at the largest bandicoot of them all.' And breaking into the third person with a touch of theatre, 'He hasn't yet had a taste of Ananthan Pillai. Sir Mohammad Usman and Sir C. Shankaran Nair? Peanuts!' The people of Palghat looked upon the two Knights as great brown feudatories, but here was a more intimidating imperial monster with a crooked sceptre. However, their fear was tempered with gratitude: the rat hunt had resulted in the unearthing of quintals of hoarded sugar which Muthalif was selling in trickles on the black market.

After the incident a parallel epidemic of fear began in the alleys of the black market. Shopkeepers made secret overtures to Ananthan Pillai, offering him money and the best whores in town; but he spurned them all.

*

Venugopalan's grandmother said, 'I don't like the look of things. I think one needs be kind even while doing justice.' The grandsons, Venugopalan and his brothers aged fourteen and twelve, laughed. The old one often spoke the language of a pastoral past; how could she understand a contemporary bacillus? Besides, did they not participate in Ananthan Pillai's flag marches!

Ananthan Pillai broke open hoarders' cellars and ancient manors, he fumigated them and in these dank citadels perished legions of rats and bandicoots. Those which fled down the sewers were chased by the relentless fumes. At the height of the pogrom Ananthan Pillai battered down the carved doors of Ganapathy's temple and stood facing the deity with the gas gun. The events that followed are shrouded in mystery; it is said that a single bejewelled rat emerged from behind the idol and, scurrying out into the street, vanished in smoke. There were no witnesses, but people in nearby shops heard the screams of Velayuthan Chettiyar, the priest, as he beat his head on the stone idol and died... The plague war went on in this fashion for two months. After his frugal lunch, Ananthan Pillai would recline in a lounge chair in the plague shop. These were the hours of truce. He would lounge with the plague register resting on his belly and the pretty inoculatress seated beside him. When the siesta ended, Ananthan Pillai would hoist himself out of the lounge chair and twirling his hooked wand, walk up and down the street, furrowing through a sea of bacilli. In these two months his storm-troop had grown to two hundred. It was a mighty formation if you considered the size of the old imperial armies of Palghat, which seldom crossed a hundred, yet had made the emperors invincible; the people of Palghat especially cherished the memory of one such emperor, Kombi Achchan of the Knives. He was known by this appellation, since he practised a peculiar variation of the emperor's craft. After his breakfast of gruel every morning he would walk about the streets—the sovereigns of Palghat were too poor to afford horses—and behead the first citizen who caught his fancy. It was a head a day, but it produced stability in the empire and stability helped progress and development. That was the golden age of Palghat and even after the Sultan's invasion and eventual annexation by the British, the people of Palghat recalled the time of the head a day with nostalgia. It was to this ancient memory that Ananthan Pillai related,he was the New Emperor of the Hooked Sceptre,the dispeller of rats.

The death toll rose to three hundred. The plague policemen broke into the houses of the dead and flung out bronze utensils with a horrendous clatter. They caught hold of the uninoculated ones and hung them head down from the rafters. They exhumed bodies not accounted for in the plague register, cut off their testicles and breasts which they marinated with turmeric and lime and strung between the avenue trees in gruesome garlands of meat. After this they put seals on the bodies, daubed serial numbers in tar, stuck on grotesquely smiling masks of cardboard, and carried them off for their second burial to the strains of a solemn death march by the police band.

After the five hundredth death, as if on cue, the bacilli left the town and moved on. The plague police now numbered five hundred. And though the bacilli had fled and the rats had recovered, Ananthan Pillai still lounged in his chair, darker and stouter. The hair on his nape grayed silver, and that on his ear lobes, frizzed, standing out like antlers. The emperors of old, and the police inspectors who succeeded them, all had taken tributes from the people, and had taken their women as well. But Ananthan Pillai did neither, and for these reasons the citizens treasured his benevolent terror.

*

The events about to be narrated here will probably seem unconnected with those narrated in the preceding pages. This is a correct assumption; here is no sequence, as in all history...

Years had gone by, Ananthan Pillai turned eighty. He no longer sat in the plague shop. No one knew exactly where he did, but it was vaguely suspected that he now rested within the old Sultan's fort. There were celebrations in town to mark his eightieth birthday, fetes and rallies at which activists lauded his great captaincy in the war of man against bacillus. But the truth was that none of those who spoke had clear memories of the epidemic. Ananthan Pillai was not present at these ceremonies, and as the years slipped by, no one saw him anymore; but as they gazed at the granite fort from a distance they were reassured that he was there. In this reassurance all Palghat observed *Dharma*, even the tradesmen with cellars beneath their shops...

The people now computed Ananthan Pillai's age at a hundred and twenty. The plague police now numbered five thousand. The regular policemen, a harried lot, cringed before this new phalanx. The epidemic itself was so distanced, that it had passed into the realm of myth. Even the plague policemen harboured no more enmity towards the rats. The little rodents, crinkling their snouts flirtatiously, pattered all over the camps, and the plague policemen caressed their glistening coats.

*

Venugopalan's grandmother was long dead, and he himself had become a great-grandfather. On his great-grandson's seventh birthday, the old man decided that he should buy gold ear-studs for the child. He set out after breakfast to the jeweller's shop a mile away. He had hardly walked twenty yards when he realized that he had left his purse behind, so turned back to pick it up.

'Etta!' a friendly voice called after him. Venugopalan turned, and saw that it was Raman, the plague policeman.

'Nice to see you, Raman *poleeze*!' Venugopalan said.

Raman had been the neighbourhood vegetable hawker,then like all the able-bodied men in town had enlisted in the plague police. Raman stood before Venugopalan in *khaki* fatigues and the red beret with the rooster's crest.

'Where are you off to in the morning, etta?' Raman asked.

Venugopalan explained that he was going to the jeweller to buy studs but had forgotten his purse and was going back to pick it up. Having done with these pleasantries, Venugopalan resumed his walk but the plague policeman barred his way.

Raman asked,'How's everybody at home?'

'Very well.'

'Nanikutty?'

'She is fine.'

'Has Kamalakshi come of age?'

'She has. Why! She's a big woman.'

'Has aunt Dakshayani seen the last of her periods?'

'Well, these women. They all go through menopause.'

'How's the crop this time?'

'Not so good.'

'What's the manure? Cowdung or shit?'

'Shit.'

As the questions multiplied, an unreasoning fear gripped Venugopalan. What was there to be afraid of, Raman was their neighbourhood policeman, once upon a time he had come to their house carrying potatoes and peas, and had never haggled over the prices. Yet he had the headgear on, the rooster's crested beret of the plague police. Venugopalan felt that he was filling in a government questionnaire and was intimidated. He turned to go but Raman barred his way a second time.

'I shall sing a song,' Raman said.

'As you wish,' Venugopalan said helplessly.

Capering a little, Raman broke into incredible doggerel, 'mickle, pickle, tickle, dickle...' It went on, the doggerel and the capering, until, drawn into a current of subservience, Venugopalan began keeping beat. *In the last moments of clarity left to him before his life ended, Venugopalan would recall this keeping beat, a trivial appeasement in the vain hope of reprieve. But there would be no reprieve and he might as well have spared himself the indignity...*

When the doggerel ended, Venugopalan reasoned, 'Raman *poleeze*, now let me go on my way.'

'Where to?' Raman asked.

Incredulously Venugopalan found himself repeating his story—all about the child's birthday and the ear-studs... Ending the narrative, he sought the plague policeman's permission to go, 'So may I, Raman *poleeze*?'

'You may not,' the policeman said.

Venugopalan paused in bewilderment. Raman said, 'Now that

you have set foot on this path, and chosen the direction, you will have to walk to the very end of it.'

'I shall do that,' Venugopalan said weakly, 'but let me go and collect my purse.'

'You shall not do that. There is no turning back.'

True, reasoned Venugopalan, *he had chosen this path. But where does the road begin, and where does it end*? Raman assured him that there would be plague policemen at every fork in the road and they would guide him. Venugopalan now tried to work on their familiarity. 'Raman, *poleeze*,' he said, 'after all we're old friends. Remember the days when we bought your potatoes and peas...'

Raman ignored this. 'Walk!' he commanded.

'Where to?' Venugopalan asked in despair.

'Forward!'

It struck Venugopalan that this could not be true but was merely a hilarious nightmare, a prank of the amiable vegetable hawker. With a sense of release, Venugopalan laughed, and laughing, turned to walk homewards. The next moment Raman had him by the scruff of the neck. He violently pushed him the other way.

'Bastard!' Raman bellowed. 'Walk on, you bastard!'

Without a word Venugopalan walked. Briefly he looked back towards his house and caught a glimpse of petrified faces behind the windows.

Venugopalan walked on. Presently he became aware of many more people on the road who walked along, silent, unsmiling. Perhaps, he thought, these people too had come out of their houses on trivial missions, to buy ear-studs or to pawn a bangle, to feast at a friend's or to buy vegetables or to fornicate; but whatever their first steps were, now they marched on in concert, drawn by the awesome mystery of the road. After an hour Venugopalan encountered a second plague policeman who waved him on to the road that branched off from the one he was on. Further down was a crossing, again the walkers were separated and turned along different ways. More turns and crossings, more silent people. Though he was tired and hungry, Venugopalan was strangely satisfied that his people were no longer the anarchical rabble they once were, but had learnt to march in step.

It was noon, and Venugopalan remembered the child's birthday feast, and tears welled up in his eyes. A tufted Chettiyar, one of the walkers, turned on him with a reprimand, 'Walk on properly!'

'And what about you?' Venugopalan protested. 'You're the one who's talking.'

Venugopalan was angry the Chettiyar had disrupted the rhythm of the march. But the next instant he was dumbfounded by what seemed an epiphany.

The Chettiyar's springy tuft grew and changed into a rooster's crest, the insignia of the plague policeman! So they were everywhere, in impenetrable disguise, and there was no knowing who they were. Venugopalan's head spun.

'Bastard!' the plague policeman spoke through clenched teeth, 'wipe your tears away.'

Venugopalan obeyed; in the brief instant in which he dried his tears, the plague policeman had changed form again, in place of the Chettiyar now walked a bent old woman. Terror gripped Venugopalan.

By afternoon he came to where a narrow lane branched off from the road, and a policeman waved him onto this. There were no other marchers, the loneliness was oppressive. At the end of the lane was a library, and this, Venugopalan concluded, was the end of his journey. He recognized the library as the one for which, in his youth, he had raised money. Yet a dream-like unfamiliarity seemed to have come over it. As Venugopalan stood baffled before the building, a pretty young woman came out to receive him. She took him into the deserted lobby, and, pointing to the stacks inside, said, 'We have a magnificent collection.'

Venugopalan felt a tinge of pride; years ago this had been *his* library. He followed the girl into the stack room.

'Can I have a glass of water?' he said, 'I am very thirsty.'

'Would you like a snack as well?'

'Yes, thank you.'

She went off at a brisk trot into one of the long corridors that radiated from the lobby, and Venugopalan sank into the cushioned depths of a sofa; he felt comforted and reassured. The pretty girl, smiling and concerned, was soon back with a tray laden with an assortment of eatables and a large jar of fruit juice. She laid the tray on a table and sat beside him.

'It must have been a long walk,' she said.

The food restored him, and he said, 'God bless you, my child.'

He was curious to know more about her, and was pleasantly surprised when he discovered that she was Savitri, the daughter of a feudal aristocrat he knew very well. Her family had produced a line of religious scholars, and was known for its gentleness and piety. Venugopalan sat talking about her family and his and was greatly relaxed. 'Now, my child,' he said, 'I must go.'

'Go? Where?'

'Home, of course.'

'But how can you? Don't you have to read these books?'

Venugopalan looked at her, uncomprehending, lost. 'Do you, do you really suggest...?'

'Of course I do,' she said, her voice tranquil. 'You have to read up as many books as you can. We will give you time till noon tomorrow.

His fevered gaze scanned the stacks, as he listened to the tranquil voice going on, 'You can rest after twelve tomorrow. Lunch is at one, and at two the examination.'

'Examination?'

'Yes. What else will you be reading all these books for?'

Venugopalan lost hold of his thoughts, his brain felt like a trough of saline soaking his reason. He found himself asking, 'Does the question paper offer choice?'

'Plenty of choice. Don't be nervous.'

She rose. 'I have work to attend to inside,' she said. 'Don't hesitate to call me if you need anything and, if you feel like, you can begin reading straightaway. You have the freedom of the library.'

Savitri disappeared through a swing door. Venugopalan was alone; this was the library he had raised money to build, and this was the daughter of the kindly scholar, whose discourses he had often listened to. Surely reality was distorted somewhere, a gentle sleight of sorcery perhaps, some innocent prank of magic. He would break the spell, he laughed aloud.

He got up to go home. But the locked exit door was no illusion. A mistake perhaps, he told himself, and walked down the corridors in search of another door. Then he saw an open toilet, its window without bars. It was undignified slipping out this way, yet he hauled himself out through the window. He landed in a strange place which looked like a school playground, full of swings and slides; a number of children between six and ten were at play. Venugopalan walked towards them. As he approached, the play froze, and the children seemed to pin him down with their unwavering stares. Then one of the children gave a word of command, 'Get him!' The rest, screaming together, began the attack. A piece of brick hit Venugopalan's forehead, starting a tiny trickle of blood. Venugopalan turned and ran with the children after him. He tripped and fell, and blacked out for a moment; when he came to, there was a little child straddling his prostrate body, hammering the back of his neck with a crooked little walking stick. Venugopalan shook the child off, and as the little one rolled over, rose to his feet. Then he saw the child's face, and cried in agony, 'It's you, Unni?'

This was a child from his neighbourhood, Sitalakshmi's son, of an age with his own great-grandchild. Unni still gripped the stick. Venugopalan gathered him up in his arms, and kissed his forehead. 'My child, my child,' he said, 'what has come over you?' The boy began sobbing, like any child of seven, and the stick dropped from his hand. Venugopalan picked it up and gave it back to the child. Setting him down on the ground, he said, 'Now, my son, go and play.'

Unni walked away, his head bent in a child's embarrassment, and joined his playmates waiting at a distance. As soon as he fell in with them he turned towards Venugopalan, the manic glint returned to his eyes, and twirling the crooked stick, he charged at him. The children screamed together, 'Get him!'

'Children, my children,' Venugopalan cried, and then, giving up, turned back towards the library. He hauled himself in through the window, and once inside, bolted it. Shaken and struggling for breath he walked back along the corridors. He was relieved to find Savitri waiting for him. 'Ah, my child,' Venugopalan said. Savitri did not return the greeting, but strode towards him with measured, menacing steps. Holding him up by his collar she lunged at his genitals with her bent knee. Venugopalan bellowed in pain. Pushing him down amid the stacks, the daughter of a gentle aristocracy, the hymn-chanters, said, 'Read, bastard!'

Without offering further resistance, Venugopalan began to read. Soon he was consoling himself with the thought, *reading is the acquisition of more knowledge after all. It is for my own good.* He read well into the night, and when in the depths of the library a clock chimed twelve, he lay down on the carpet, and curling up like a kitten, went into deep sleep. He dreamed. Little children scurried in his dream, children of six and seven, with studs of gold on their ears, and smiles on their tender lips. Venugopalan cried in his sleep, he started awake, and sat up and cried, then like a child, cried himself to sleep again. The dream repeated, as did the waking; in the morning when he rose his mind was full of the peace of children. He sat down to read again. At twelve noon, he closed his books and rested till lunch. The lunch was sumptuous, a real feudal spread; and Venugopalan ate as if it was his great-grandson's birthday feast. At two, the examination began. He had two-and-a-half hours to answer the questions.

Venugopalan sat alone and began to write. There was no one else taking the examination. Words seemed to float out of him like thistledown, briefly their insides lighting with sense, dulling again into grey opacity. Now he was chasing them over a parched desert, faltering and falling, and painfully rising. The parched illusion ended and he was cruelly back at his desk. Alone, seeking the answers all alone... Savitri came in to collect his paper, 'Now relax. The verdict will be handed down at six.'

'Verdict?' Venugopalan asked, aghast.

'The verdict of the examination.'

*

The verdict was given at six. Venugopalan was to be hanged by the neck till dead. Trying futilely to break out of a tiny cell where he could neither lie down nor stand, he merely bruised his forehead against the door. *No,* he said, *I shall not struggle nor bruise any limb. I shall not cry, for my tears would only make my insides sodden like the sidewalks of Sultanpet.*

At midnight there was a tap on the door and someone peeped in through the vent. Venugopalan choked as he recognized the caller, 'You, my Janardhanan?'

'It's me, Gopal-etta.'

The word *etta*, it's respect and affection, touched the pools of love within, and Venugopalan's tears came in torrents.

'Don't cry, Gopal-etta,' Janardhanan consoled.

Janardhanan had once been his protégé, one of the numberless youngsters who had followed him on fund-raising rounds for the library. Venugopalan wondered what he was doing here.

'Well,' Janardhanan said, 'it's an awkward job, I can tell you so. It's tugging at the rope.'

'O Janardhanan...' Venugopalan began, then stopped, overcome.

'Feel grateful,' Janardhanan said. 'It's me after all. Isn't it comforting to have an old friend for one's hangman?'

Venugopalan did not know why he said so, but he replied, 'Yes, it's comforting.'

'Aren't we in it together for a public cause, Gopal-etta? Each one has to put up with a little inconvenience.'

'One has to.'

'Remember the days when we raised the funds, don't you?'

'I remember.'

'Now go to sleep, Gopal–etta. See you at dawn.'

*

Early the next morning, as he ascended the scaffold, Venugopalan had no fear. There was only light within him, a deluge of light shining over memories of things which began with the squat man with the crooked walking stick. He did not see the spectators, or his weeping kinsmen who stood among them. Nor did he know that his great-grandson had left the abandoned birthday feast and walked down the street in search of him. The child lost his way and wandered on and on, through strange streets and alleys. Men who marched silently pushed him out of their way. Then the grim rhythmic march passed over him, rhythmic footfalls squeezed his eyes out. A scavenging bird swooped down and pecked at the eyeballs. With his last breath the little one cried out, 'Grandfather, it's dark.'

FANTASY
AND
ROMANCES

Anachronisms

'Venerable Judges,' the supplicant said, 'may you in your wisdom know the sorrow of a father. What crime could my son have committed, he who has barely left his childhood behind? Or what is the crime committed by one of such tender age that you cannot forgive?'

'Your son's crime is treason. He has defiled this nation's hallowed articles.'

'Wise ones, I rocked him as an infant in my arms, and soothed him with lullabies. Let me place before you those memories.'

'Prosecutor! Read the indictment...'

The bald man stroked his goatee and massaged his forehead, he batted his eyelids rapidly in improvised therapy, yet the surging tumult within his head showed no sign of calming. It was the gush of memories, and today they were rising to intolerable pressure. He bent his head in pain and sat thus for a long while. When he lifted his gaze to look round again, the room was filled with murky fog.

'Krupskaya,' he said, speaking to himself, 'if you were here now you could have seen this for yourself. And you would have believed my story.'

This was the fog of memory, and it slithered out of his nose and ears. Its rapid spiralling felt like excretion, libidinous.

'Krupskaya,' he said, 'I wish you could see how it fills my room.'

All this was happening in a street in a Parisian suburb where whores and pimps and painters kept their festering tenancies. He feared that the fog, once it filled the room, might soon spill outdoors. The street was full of fugitives from every time and cause, and people so embittered were capable of much cynicism and mockery. If they caught sight of the fog, these spirals of his memory, he would be undone. He rose and slammed the window shut.

In 1917, October, according to the old calendar — he tried to re-run his memory. A vicious whorl of fog slid out of his left ear. It was murkier than the usual grey, and streaked red as with unclean and congealed blood. It spun forward to the closed window and knocked on the panes. He screamed in alarm.

Could he have stopped it? He was not sure, it had happened all too suddenly. The red tinted spiral heaved up against the window and struck it with solid force. The window came off its hinges and fell noisily onto the street. The fog now issued forth with renewed violence haemorrhaging through ear and nose and the genital and anal orifices. Even this did not relieve its pressure, and it pierced the bald pate and rose like a whale's spout. Yet it did not hurt, for the rupture was not one of flesh and bone, it was *non-material*. He was a dialectical materialist, he reminded himself, and this was an outlet of the *spirit*! He was embarrassed that this should have happened to him, and desperately hoped that none of the expatriate revolutionaries would discover his secret. Presently he came to terms with the steady faucet in the head, it was smoother than the other outlets. The fog soon ceased coming out of them, but rose from the vent in the skull in an enormous fountain. He gave himself up to its sensuality. A band of street children appeared at the window, they stood gazing into the room.

'A whale!' one of the children cried.

The bald man was annoyed. 'Get lost, sons of counter-revolutionaries!'

That did not scare the children away. 'A silly whale with a goatee!' they chorused.

Now he had a sudden and disconcerting vision. He saw a vast sea, and saw himself afloat on it, his head pumping, and his giant tail flailing the water. Dotting the sea was a school of whales: his old comrades as well as class enemies. He knew this was the work of the children, their irresponsible sorcery.

'Children, my children,' he called out helplessly, 'turn me into a man again!'

Chattering and laughing, the children scampered away. He howled in pain, 'Krupskaya, Krupskaya!'. *She was not here.* With a stab of pain he set right another memory. She had not become his wife but married one of Petrograd's wealthy tradesmen instead. The sea grew chill.

An officer from the Commissariat of Health came up to the window and peeped in. 'What's going on here?'

'I have turned into a whale,' the bald man sobbed.

'Aren't you ashamed to cry? Hurry up, and turn into a man again.'

After the officer walked away from the window, the whale lay on the water a little longer, crying. Then convulsing himself from snout to tail, he resumed his human shape. The effort tired him. He rested awhile, unmindful of the fog that kept billowing through his invisible vent.

The fog was seeping freely into the street now, and he heard coughs and sneezes from the neighbouring apartments.

A young gendarme came up and tapped on the window-frame with his baton. A mere stripling in uniform; the bald man was distressed that he could be so disrespectful to the old.

'Go away!' he said.

This merely amused the gendarme. 'Why should I go away? I am trying to help. If you sit here indulging in memories of *non-happenings*, you're sure to fall hopelessly ill.'

'I can look after myself. Go away.'

The gendarme became coercive. 'I warn you, out of concern. It is not my responsibility to be concerned, but stopping the fog certainly is. If you don't stop it yourself, I will have to take steps as a policeman.'

He was joined by another gendarme and then by a corporal.

'What's going on here?' the corporal demanded of the gendarmes.

'The fog,' the gendarmes said.

The corporal looked round, and sniffed the air. 'True,' he said. 'This is against the law. The neighbourhood will suffocate. Old man, why did you do this?'

But the fog was beyond the bald man's control; it rose freely from his vent.

'Stop him!' the corporal told the gendarmes, who leapt in through the window and handcuffed the bald man.

'What's you name?' they asked.

'Vladimir Ilyich.'

'Your trade?'

'Interpreting Marxism in the era of Imperialism.'

The gendarmes smiled indulgently, 'You'll get over it. Now come with us.'

*

The bald man sat cooling his heels in the police cell, and began all over again with his memories. *Vladimir Ilyich, that's my name. I...I...*

The stripling policeman came to the door of the cell with a bowl of liquor. 'Here, this is for you,' he said.

The bald man hesitated. 'Intruding urchin! What guarantee is there that you are not trying to poison me?'

The gendarme smiled. 'Poison you? Why should anyone poison you?'

The bald man did not hide his contempt and irritation. 'Don't pretend. You do know the reasons.'

The young gendarme's tone grew stern and business-like, 'Drink it.'

He passed the bowl through the bars of the prison door; the bald man took a tentative sip, it was good Russian vodka. The French gendarmerie had a sense of propriety after all.

The vent was now beginning to hurt, the congestion mounting; an uneasy chill seized his head. The bald man drained the goblet in one draught.

'Now sleep,' the gendarme said. 'We dissolved a sleeping pill in the vodka. It will help you get over these troublesome memories.'

The gendarme walked away; and the bald man sat back in his cell, spewing fog. The sleeping pill, the policeman's betrayal, caused him to rage impotently; the sedative was playing havoc with the dates of his precious private history.

1917, October, the guns of the battleship were trained on the Winter Palace and he was exhorting the seamen to fire. Wars are won or lost by the single soldier, who blindly plunges into action or turns back in as illogical a panic. This solitary hireling was now dithering; the cannons did not fire. 'Sailors, brothers! If this revolution does not take place I will have to wander again, a fugitive, in some strange European city. Fire!' But no one fired. The revolution did not happen.

Outside, there was a blinding flash of lightning, it pierced the walls and bruised his eyes. Thunder ripped open the skies and tore through the bowels of the earth, and the opiate grew heavy like a tombstone. The rain poured down washing the fog away from the street in muddy torrents.

*

When the bald man woke up, he felt he had slept for days and nights together. The gendarmes had given him a cell-mate while he slept, a slim, brown youngster with long hair and beard and dressed in a roomy cassock.

The face was oddly familiar.

The bald man felt his pate and his ear and nostril. The newcomer smiled. 'I can see the vent in your head. True, it is invisible to ordinary men, because it is *non-material*.'

The bald man wondered who this youngster was who could so uncover his spiritual privacy.

'Stop talking foolishly,' he said defensively. The newcomer smiled again. 'Do not be afraid,' he said. 'The fog is not coming out, at least for the time being. When I came in here there were still little wisps of it.'

'You,' the bald man said, 'you saw them?'

'I did,' the young man's voice was full of sympathy. 'They were full of dates.'

'Dates?'

'Yes, the dates of *happenings* that never happened.'

The bald man was lost in thought. 'Is the street,' he asked after a while, 'still overhung with the fog?'

'The rain must have washed it clean.'

'I suppose so.'

'But why do you feel guilty? If it is not your fog, it will be someone else's. There has not been a single day when the street was free from fog. Look...'

The young man held out his hands, there were holes in the palms, as though someone had driven nails through them, the disfigurement of old injury.

'Good grief!' the bald man said. 'What is this?'

'It is an old story. Again, a story of *non-happenings*. I used to be a carpenter in Jerusalem when they nailed me to a wooden cross but my Father and Mother bribed the centurions and took me down. Surely, you have heard of my Father?'

'No.'

'No?' The carpenter lifted his gaze towards the ceiling of the prison cell and called out aloud, 'Father, Father!'

This frenetic cry disturbed the bald man unreasonably. As if in response to the cry, the corporal appeared at the door. 'What are you shouting for?'

'I never called you,' the carpenter said.

'I suppose not,' the corporal said. 'I know I am not your old man.'

The carpenter's eyes gleamed. 'Policeman,' he said, 'get thee behind me!'

Blaspheming heartily the corporal walked back to his chamber.

'Go on,' the bald man said.

'Yes, I remember. My Father and Mother bribed the centurions. Then they prised out the nails and got me down from the cross. The physicians ministered to me for many months, until I could walk about. But these stigmata...'

'Hold on,' the bald man said. 'Did you say the cross? What was that?'

The carpenter drew the sign of the cross on the floor with his forefinger. 'I too get these memories,' he said, 'of *happenings* that never happened; and on such occasions the fog comes out of these holes in my palms and my feet. If they had killed me on the cross, I might have begun a religion.'

'How could you? When one is killed what more can one do?'

'You have a point there.'

'That is the point. Death is a happening, a happening that *happens*.'

The carpenter was silent for a while, and then said, 'It is for the same reason that sometimes I trust in happenings that never were. Ah, what was I saying? If they had killed me on the cross, I would have founded a religion. There would have been no one like you unfamiliar with the sign of the cross.'

The bald man was amused and spoke without reverence, 'It's no great loss not to know the sign of the cross.'

The carpenter reddened with pentecostal fire. 'You talk most foolishly. What is a man worth if he does not know the sign of the cross?'

'Some presumption!' It was the turn of the bald man to be angry. 'Do you know of the sickle-and-hammer?'

'Yes, work tools.'

The bald man laughed disdainfully. 'This then is the level of your awareness. If you do not know, I shall instruct you. Listen, you ignorant nut!'

'Mind your words, old clod!'

'You dare call me a clod, you urchin?'

The carpenter sprang up and held him by the goatee and out came a scrawl of fog, almost involuntarily. 'If my revolution had *happened*,' the bald man said, 'I would have had you shot as a counter-revolutionary.'

At this the carpenter fell upon the bald man and began boxing his ears.

'Stop it!' cried a woman who appeared at the door of the cell. 'What madness is this!'

'This clod here,' said the carpenter to the woman, 'hasn't heard of the cross, yet he makes fun of it.'

'Enough of the cross!' she said. She seemed to cast a spell over the carpenter. He quietened. She was pretty and young. 'Who's she?' enquired the bald man.

'My cousin,' the carpenter said, 'Mary.'

'Listen Mary, my child,' the bald man said. 'I didn't start the fight. He has not heard of the sickle-and-hammer, and yet he sniggers at it. Know, my child, that the sickle-and-hammer is the emblem of the international proletariat. Had the cowards shown better sense and fired at the Winter Palace, there would have been no one today unfamiliar with the sickle-and-hammer. Had they fired, I would have been the Chairman of Russia's Council of Ministers...'

His eyes welled with tears. 'The Chairman...' he sobbed. 'They didn't fire. Cowards! Dogs!'

The woman understood nothing, yet she felt sympathy for the bald man. 'Uncle,' she said, 'please do not cry.'

'My Krupskaya! Today even she is not here beside me.'

At this the carpenter burst into offensive laughter. 'Now who is the ignorant nut? Krupskaya never left you for the simple reason that she was never with you. You never met. Don't you realize, you ignorant cretin, that you lived together only in the old calendar, the chronicle of *non-happenings*?'

The woman was mystified by the conversation, yet she said, 'Forget Krupskaya, uncle. Look at me...' She began unbuttoning her shift. Pretty breasts spilled out, pink-nippled, and with blue and dreamy veins. The breasts bore the marks of clawing, work of diverse hands.

'Look at all this, uncle...' The shift reached down to her ankles and she unbuttoned it all the way. The garment fell apart, revealing her pale navel and fair thighs. The bald man looked on hungrily.

'I shall make you happy, uncle!'

The carpenter turned pale. 'Mary!' he said in vain deterrence.

'You shut up,' she said. 'A little while ago, I had to sleep with the Commissioner of the gendarmerie for a promise of your release.'

The carpenter's shame was deep and he said, 'You unbutton your shift, then you knock, and it opens.'

'Ungrateful one!'

She turned towards the bald man again, 'Something tells me you are a good man, uncle. They must have picked you up for some honest crime. Burglary, pimping...'

'Oh no!'

'Why do you indulge in false humility? You are a good man, a burglar or a pimp. I am a whore, and a whore's inner voice never lies. Please save this cousin of mine. They nailed him to the cross once upon a time and our family pooled together its scanty savings to bribe the centurions. But that has made him crazy, he wanders from town to town talking of the crucifixion and the politics of crucifixion. But who on earth is interested in a *non-happening*? It is true he was cruelly impaled, and it must have hurt him terribly. But what use is it to talk about pain to those who have not known it? And then, it is not sensible to talk of the same thing day in and day out.'

'Will you stop it, ignorant woman?' the carpenter said in a rage. 'He too is one like me, except that he has the sickle-and-hammer instead of the cross. He too, like me, spends his days and nights talking its politics.'

'The sickle-and-hammer?' the woman asked.

'Yes. The emblem of the international proletariat. I interpret Marxism in the era of Imperialism.'

The woman was not interested in Imperialism. She said, 'Uncle, put some sense into my cousin. People call him the fellow of the cross, they do so in derision, and most of them avoid him. I can endure this disgrace no longer.'

The bald man moved towards the prison door. The woman put her hands in through the bars and stroked him beneath his navel. With great dexterousness she unbuttoned his pants and slipped in her hand, stroking him into arousal. The carpenter pushed her hand away. But in that instant the bald man's ageing nakedness tumbled out and was spent.

'Button up,' said the carpenter in disgust. Then calming down, he continued, 'She is crazy. Don't waste your time listening to her.'

The bald man felt his insides churning, and his feeble passion spent, he collapsed to the floor. As he did so, his restraint gone, the vent once again gave way. The carpenter laughed but the woman cried out in alarm, 'Uncle, you too have the sickness of the fog?' She beat her breast and began wailing, 'God, god! How this fog tires me!'

'Get a hold on yourself, my friend,' the carpenter told the bald man. 'I suspect they will free both of us in a short while.'

'No, not me. I am the leader of the world revolution. Capitalism will not spare me.'

'The police are indulgent towards revolutions which have not *happened*. They will not keep you, so restrain this fog of yours and tidy up your pate. We can rest under a bridge or on the waterfront and let off fog to our hearts' content. We might upset too many people here: the gendarmes, this foolish woman...'

The bald man assented reluctantly. It hurt him deeply to be told that Capitalism had not even recognized him as an enemy.

Slowly the fog abated, and the woman, still in tears, walked away from the door.

*

'Wise ones, I stand before your Seat of Justice, and cry. Oh, why is it that you do not heed me? Grant reprieve to my child once, just this once. Mercy will redeem you.'

'He rants before our Seat of Justice. Silence him!'

'Wise ones, stay your hand awhile. That which you exercise justice for is unreal. It has not happened. So are your statutes, they were not written. Do not take a life for what has never been.'

'Your Lordships, the charges have ben proved beyond doubt. The Prosecution prays for justice.'

'Alas, Wise Ones...'

The bald man and the carpenter were free now; they found their way into a tavern and sat down with mugs of ale. Over his drink the bald man spent much time wondering what the cross was, and why its very mention agitated the carpenter. In his mind its erosion as an emblem was strangely mixed up with the erosion of the sickle-and-hammer, and once again he laid the blame on the single hireling who dithered, the solitary coward who unmade history. If only the trigger had been pulled, a hundred others would have followed suit, and the revolution enshrined him in history. He would have been clinking glasses, handwrought crystal, with kings and emperors; his every word, even casual indiscretions, incoherences, would have found their way into books of infallible theory. But today he was condemned to flit from tavern to tavern seeking out fellow expatriates, and bear their ridicule and reluctant hospitality. In bitter regret once again, the October of 1917 spiralled out of his vent in a wisp of fog.

A dance was on in the tavern; three girls gyrating obscenely and slipping out of their garments. The revue pleased the bald man and the carpenter.

'This reminds me of my Krupskaya,' said the bald man with a gentle tinge of guilt.

'I too am reminded,' said the carpenter. 'Satan showed me a number of women.'

'Is he still around?'

'Who?'

'Satan, didn't you say?'

The carpenter giggled, 'But Satan is the Devil.'

'Is he a counter-revolutionary?'

'Oh, no, just a devil.'

'It doesn't matter. Tell me where he is.'

'He isn't around.'

'And the women?'

The carpenter fell awhile into brooding silence, then spoke, 'I am struck by the story of your revolution, its interminable boredom. So is it with the story of the Devil and the women. I must confess it is part of my fog. But see what is going on...'

In the midst of the dancing slatterns there appeared a middle-aged man in battle fatigues. He wore a moustache, an absurd and abrupt rectangle of clipped hair, giving his face a kind of cretinous gravity. Linking hands with the girls and capering briskly, he imitated them with obscene movements of his behind.

The tavern was full of people: masons and mill-hands, whores and pimps and painters. All of them greeted the revue with raucous delight.

'I know him,' the carpenter said.

'Do you?'

'He claims to be an enemy of the Jews. You see, I had trouble with the Jews myself, and he took advantage of this to befriend me. But I told him, get thee behind me.'

'What's his name?'

'Adolf.'

Adolf danced on, and as the music grew vigorous his cheeks puffed and his eyes bulged. Then suddenly black smoke blew out of his nostrils.

'Is he smoking a cigar?' the bald man enquired.

'No,' the carpenter said, 'it's the fog. Only it is dirtier than ours. Look at the whorl, it is 1939.'

'When was that?'

'Poor nut! He planned to start a war that year. A mad, mad war, it would make you split your sides with laughter.'

'I suppose it didn't *happen*?'

'Of course it didn't. That explains the fog. Look at that whorl now, the year he was supposed to build a large oven to incinerate the Jews.'

A fat stonemason moved to their table. 'How much gratis entertainment there is in this world!' the mason said. 'Each clown who presumes to lead humanity ends up blowing putrid soot from his nose and ears to amuse fools like me.' The mason slapped the bald man on the thigh, gulped his ale and guffawed, and then, began to sneeze.

'Stop it, you ruffian!' he yelled at Adolf. 'Your fog is dirtier today.'

'Not everyone likes Adolf's fog,' the carpenter said. 'Sometimes it smells of shit.'

'Right now it's like a fart,' the bald man said.

'But Adolf has delusions. He thinks the smell is a big draw.'

'It's not altogether a delusion. Adolf has a bit of truth there.'

'True,' the carpenter intervened, 'one never knows the mind of the multitude.'

'The multitude? Well I know the mind of the *broad masses*.'

'Stop it!' cried the mason and rose to assault Adolf. The tavern keeper too advised Adolf to restrain his fog. But there was no way Adolf could stop suddenly overflowing with the soot of memory. The naked girls came to his help, stopping his orifices with their palms, but it only caused the pressure to mount within his ducts. Adolf moaned aloud in distress, and defecated onto the hands of the girls. They raised their hands, stained with the excrement, chanting, 'Seig Heil!'

'What's that?' the bald man asked.

'I think it's a battle cry of sorts,' the carpenter said. 'It's part of the revue. Every time he is done with his pissing and shitting the girls chant it.'

The fat mason was listening to their conversation. 'It's nothing special,' he said. 'After the fart and the shit and the piss every leader expects to be cheered. And people invariably oblige him.'

'You can't generalize,' the bald man said. 'It's not true of the proletariat.'

'Who are you to say this?' the mason asked.

'The leader of the working class.'

'Just a leader, aren't you? I'm the real thing, the working class.'

'I'm...'

'Shut up!'

The mason was a formidable hulk, and spoiling for a fight. The bald man decided that discretion was the better part of revolution.

Now Mary stormed into the tavern. 'Aren't you men ashamed to be watching this obscenity?' she said, and led the carpenter away. The bald man followed them.

They were wandering down the street, when an automobile pulled up beside them. Peeping out of the car a bearded man with a sumptuous thatch of hair hailed the bald man, 'Vladimir Ilyich!'

'Greetings!' the bald man said obsequiously.

'I reached Paris yesterday, and was looking for you all over the place. It is really fortunate I ran into you here. I shall make it brief: you needn't waste time writing that commentary.'

'I needn't?' the bald man was alarmed.

'No. Because I haven't written the source book. The New York *Tribune* has confirmed me as its London correspondent. Comfortable salary and perks. Why should I drive myself to death writing four volumes of *Das Kapital?*'

'Does that mean,' asked the bald man, on the verge of a breakdown, 'that I am no longer the interpreter of Marxism in the era of Imperialism?'

'You must be raving mad! If there is no Marxism where is the question of its needing an interpreter?'

The bald man stood paralyzed awhile and when he got a hold on himself, beat his breast and raised a lament in the street.

'Karl, you deceiver! You have destroyed me. You never wrote that book. Then where is my commentary, my revolution!'

'Nowhere, if you want to know the truth.'

'Will the Czar continue in power? Or will it be the Government of Kerensky the lickspittle?'

Karl smothered the feeble fog which rose from his beard and said, 'Let anyone be in power. I could care less.'

'Don't you care for dialectical materialism?'

'I don't. I've got a job. Tomorrow I get back to London. See me there, they give you excellent beer in that pub near the British Museum.'

Karl drove away, yodelling an undignified song, which the bald man for a moment suspected was a parody of the *Internationale*. He clenched his fist and bellowed after the receding automobile, 'Saboteur! Counter-revolutionary!'

*

The car rolled out of sight, and the bald man, in deep depression, stood rooted on the sidewalk. Mary stood beside him, as did the carpenter caressing his stigmata.

'Come,' Mary said, tugging at the carpenter, her eyes aflame with desire. Both the bald man and the carpenter appeared too distracted to respond.

'You men ignore me,' she said. 'Fine then, I go my way,' and she went away to walk the streets.

'I am at the end of my tether. I'll crack up if I don't have a drink but I'm broke,' the bald man said.

'So am I,' the carpenter said.

They lingered on in the cold street.

'Is it night or day now?' the bald man asked.

'Neither,' the carpenter said. 'It is pure Time.'

'I don't understand.'

'Time is innocent. It is the dates which create trouble.'

The bald man repeated, 'I don't understand.'

'It doesn't matter.'

'I shall leave you now, my friend,' the bald man said. 'If I do not have a drink I'll go mad. I know of a hideout of old Russian revolutionaries. They gather most evenings, to reminisce about old struggles and the women they left behind, and drown their sorrows in ale. True, I cannot pay for my drink and they might slight me. Still they will spare me a drink, maybe even Russian vodka. Would you care to come along?'

'They might slight me too,' the carpenter said. 'I'm in no mood for it. I too have a hideout. Here are carpenters from Jerusalem who work for Parisian building contractors. These are not unfamiliar with the story of the cross and there is some sort of covenant between us about a cup of wine, which they will honour even if I can't pay.'

They parted and went their ways...

As the bald man entered, the expatriates muttered within his hearing, 'There he comes again, the pest, to cadge a drink. But he won't keep his mouth shut after the drink is poured in, he will drive us crazy with his recollections of the sailors who failed to fire.'

The bald man heard every bit of it, with a stab of pain and anger, but still walked into their midst with a forced grin. 'Waiting for me, weren't you, comrades?' This overture was greeted with glum silence. He flopped down on a chair and said, 'I can never refuse good Russian vodka. To Mother Russia!'

One of the old revolutionaries spoke, 'We shall give you the drink, you've in any case become a parasite we can't ward off. But you shall not try our patience with stories of your revolution.'

The bald man laughed aloud; the laughter rose over the morose stillness, solitary and neurotic. He would have cried had he not laughed. Laughing, he chanted, 'Workers of all countries...' There was a word-block, a mind-block. In bitter regret he said, more to himself, 'Karl, that money-hungry Jewish mercenary! When he got a job, he left without even caring to complete this slogan. In the struggle to verbalize the unwritten slogan his vent opened and spat a burst of fog like putrid phlegm... At the carpenters' rendezvous, similar resentment awaited the young man with the stigmata. 'He's back again,' railed the expatriates from Jerusalem, 'with his tedious drivel about the cross.'

*

'Prisoner in the dock! Your guilt has been proven beyond doubt. This Seat of Justice awards you the ultimate punishment. Let the arm of the State execute this decree…'

What State, O Wise and Merciful ones? It was but a delusion of history, it never existed…'

*

The bald man plodded back to his apartment, and from that untenable sanctuary peeped out through the window. The fog was a pall over the street, its stench trapped, saturated to choking. Now began an incredible revue: prisoners in weird period costumes, costumes of the near and far past, and of the future, were marched down the street by gendarmes. He called out to a gendarme, 'Where are you taking them?'

'To the clink,' the gendarme said. 'Where else?'

'And why, if I may ask?'

'It's a mopping-up job. The Commissioner has ordered the cleansing of Time.'

'The Commissioner?'

'Yes. The all-knowing and all-powerful Commissioner of the gendarmerie. He decided this morning to dispense with Historical Dates. He said the Dates were polluting the street.'

The bald man caught glimpses of faces he recognized: Katherine and Peter the Great, Attila and Genghis, Alexander of Macedonia—'I've seen them,' he said. 'In woodcuts and lithographs.'

'You'll see them no more.'

At the far end of the street presently appeared dark eddies, absurd and terrifying; the bald man wondered how the street's moderate width could hold such enormous black holes. Into these black holes disappeared both captives and captors. The lot that disappeared was followed by another wave, and another and another. The bald man said, 'Don't tell me they are...'

'Of course they are,' the gendarme said, 'historical personages from all periods.'

'Real personages?'

'As real as lithographs. That's as far as your messy reality gets anyway, a little better than *non-happenings*. All the same they pollute. The Commissioner thought enough was enough, and scored off their Dates.'

The bald man looked again towards the black holes in claustrophobia. 'I am, I am,' he whimpered, 'I too am a...'

'Historical personage?'

'Yes.'

The gendarme's eyes glinted mischievously. 'Then you wait,' he said. 'They'll come for you sooner or later.'

The bald man drew back from the window in stark terror; then, as the fog oozed again through his orifices, he remembered his history hadn't *happened*; it was a humiliating consolation, the Commissioner might not pick him after all.

I am not a historical personage, oh, I'm not, said the rhythmic din inside his head, a despairing insistent migraine; it took him apart and he flopped to the floor, threshing about with his hands and legs. Instead of hard tiles, he was splashing on water with tail and flippers. He called out in rage and infernal thirst, 'Krupskaya!' The syllables refused to jell, instead there issued the gurgling of the whale swallowing water, and from his vent rose a silver plume. All round him, dotting the waters as far as the eye could see, were whales.

The whalers came in black canoes and cast their harpoons. The shrill pain of the harpoon, and in its wake the numb, black quiet, the reprieve of nothingness. When the canoes paddled away, the whales were gone, the last wisps of mist had cleared, and the sun shone on the cleansed and infinite sea.

*

'My son, my son! On this shore I stand, your ashes in my hand. I return you to the sea, to eventless Time.'

Wind Flowers

When Chandran had packed and was ready to leave, Beeran, the caretaker of the travellers' bungalow, lost all interest in him, the only visitor who had not given him an opportunity to be a good host. After the military had wound up the hilltop camp, the travellers' bungalow which adjoined it had lost all purpose for which it had been built and attracted only occasional guests who sought pleasure in the privacy of the mountain country. The previous night Beeran had held forth on Visalakshi, describing her excellence, going over her every limb in the style of classical erotic poetry. Mistaking Chandran's silence for interest, he had waxed eloquent. But now this good-for-nothing visitor was getting ready to leave, and Beeran realized his poetry had been wasted.

Chandran rose and went to the balustrade. The dawn lit the valley below. It was just as he had seen it in his childhood, the trees blue-green in the mist, and the river showing through the areca palms.

It was to this river that you took me, Visalakshi, to show me the blood of the Namboodiri slaughtered by the Muslim rebels, blood which, the legend said, still eddied in the water. I shall presently drive back over this gravel road, the road we walked as eight-year-olds. We had walked hand in hand, and were grateful for that touch. I go without seeing you, without bidding you farewell, the ingratitude of my departure oppresses me. But perhaps it is just as well, because if we met today we might not recognize each other, and were we to look beneath the changed contours of our faces for the lost innocence of our childhood, it might cause us inconsolable sorrow. I ask myself, why then did I come here? Perhaps, it is because we revisit our innocence like a criminal the scene of his crime. Forgive me the hubris of this journey.

Chandran walked back into the room, and Beeran followed, to be of help if it was needed.

'There is nothing more to pack, Beeran,' Chandran said. 'I shall be obliged if there is some coffee.'

'By eight, shall we say?'

'Yes, thank you.'

Beeran went out of the bungalow and disappeared into the annexe that housed the pantry and the kitchen

Permit me to remember. Memory shall be our colloquy.

*

It was Chandran's first week in the Muslim school. During lunch break Visalakshi said to him, 'Do you want to come out with me?'

'Where to?' Chandran asked.

'To the areca plantation. I shall show you bunches of areca nuts.'

Chandran agreed to go with her. It was the first time he had gone anywhere but home from school. As they entered the plantation they encountered an elderly Muslim in a red sarong.

'Who is that, Visalakshi?'

'It is Mohiddeen-kaka.'

Chandran was nervous. Stories of Muslim rebels clad in red sarongs came to his mind. Mohiddeen-kaka greeted them, 'What brings you here, children?'

Chandran became even more nervous.

'This is the *Saheb's* child,' Visalakshi said. 'He wants to see the areca bunches.'

Mohiddeen-kaka laughed. 'To see the areca bunches? By all means!'

Chandran's fear of the red sarong passed.

'Child of the Major *Saheb*, aren't you?' Mohiddeen-kaka asked.

'Yes, he is,' Visalakshi said.

'And you, aren't you old Raman Nair's daughter?'

'Yes.'

Mohiddeen-kaka led them to the areca palms.

'There!' Mohiddeen-kaka pointed to the top of a palm. 'A ripe, red bunch. Shall I get it plucked for you?'

'No, thanks,' Chandran said. 'I just wanted to see it.'

It was then that they saw the big spider. It had fastened its web between two palm trees.

'Look at that, Chandran!' Visalakshi cried.

Chandran had never seen a spider so big. Mohiddeen-kaka flung a twig at it and brought it down.

'This is a bird-eater,' Visalakshi said. Chandran flinched from the spider.

It was time to be back at school.

'Let's go,' he said.

'Yes, let us.'

Visalakshi walked a few paces, and turned back. 'Look at its tail, Chandran!'

The spider was crawling away, trailing a length of tough and opaque web.

'It is not the tail,' Mohiddeen-Kaka said. 'It is the web of the evil one.'

Visalakshi picked up the web and the spider dangled helplessly at the other end. 'Chandran, are you scared?'

'Leave him,' Mohiddeen-kaka said. 'He's poisonous.'

Mohiddeen-kaka accompanied them upto the stile in the boundary fence. 'Give my *salaams* to the Major *Saheb*.'

'I shall,' Chandran said.

But Chandran could not convey that message to his father, without letting out the secret that he had wandered out of the school compound, in sly disobedience of his father's injunction. The camp on the hilltop was the authority of Occupation, and his father had forbidden him to fraternize with the children of the village. Even the teachers treated Chandran with deference, he was the child of the Major who commanded the camp.

Chandran was sent to the school of the Muslims because that was the only school around, and his father wanted Chandran to get used to children his own age. It was a school of the poor, and its teachers themselves did not have much education. To offset this Chandran had a tutor who lived with the family and taught him Browning and Coleridge.

The teachers often visited the camp to pay their respects to the Commandant. So broken was the spirit of the Muslims after their crushed rebellion, and so awesome the power of the military, that the teachers would hesitate to sit before his father. But Chandran's grandmother treated them to lavish teas, and invoked their blessings for her grandchild. Her favourite was Mohammed Haji, Chandran's class-teacher.

'He is a pious one,' she would say.

Mohammed Haji was a placid being with a round face and a corpulent body. Those were times when one could study up to the fifth standard and on the strength of that scrappy literacy train oneself to be a teacher. Mohammed Haji was one such. But this did not bother Chandran's grandmother.

'He is your teacher, your preceptor,' she would tell Chandran. 'Listen to his words of wisdom.'

The words of wisdom came in abundance. The first period at school, since it was a school for Muslims, was the teaching of the Koran. Mohammed Haji was theologian, historian and scientist rolled into one. Every day after the scripture lessons he wrote out a few problems in arithmetic on the blackboard, and then moved on to history. History was a matter of conjecture, and science daring discovery. Teaching science one day, Mohammed Haji asked, 'What is this thing that we call air? You answer, Usman!'

'Wind,' Usman said.

'Can you see the wind?'

'You cannot.'

'Then listen to me, O child of the devil! You can see the wind. Go to the riverside at noon and slant your head and watch, you can see the wind rise up like flowers.'

After this lesson, when the class broke for lunch, the children trooped to the riverside. They cocked their heads to one side, as the teacher had instructed them to, and looked over the beds of sand. And sure enough, they saw the wind flowers rise layer upon layer!

Chandran stayed behind. So did Visalakshi, working out a sum. She looked up from her book and asked him, 'Aren't you going, Chandran?'

'No.'

'Don't you want to see the wind flowers?'

Chandran contemplated saying no. But he said, 'Let us see them.'

'Then come with me.'

'But mother has told me not to go to the riverside.'

Visalakshi laughed. '*Ayyee*! What is there to be scared of? Am I not with you?'

She closed her book and came over and took his hand. 'Come, Chandran.'

When they reached the riverside, the rest of the children had left. The sands were deserted.

'Look!' Visalakshi said.

Chandran cocked his head and looked over the hot sands.

'Chandran, do you see the flowers?'

'I see them.'

Every day during lunch break, after the other children had

returned, Visalakshi took Chandran out to see the wind flowers. Chandran liked to be alone with her in the spaces of the river, to breathe her fragrance in the river breezes.

But the wind flowers disturbed him. He had read that air was invisible. At last he asked his tutor. The tutor explained to him how heat created the mirage, and recited Sanskrit poetry which described the mirage as the pond of the deluded wild deer.

Chandran did not say anything of this in class, he was reluctant to contradict Mohammed Haji. But he let Visalakshi into the secret.

'But don't tell anyone,' Chandran said.

'Why not?'

'I don't know myself. But my grandmother said something about the preceptor's blessings.'

She did not understand it either, but both realized that it would hurt their teacher if they told the others; so they decided to keep the mirage to themselves, a secret kept in tenderness and trust.

*

After these twenty years Chandran experienced the benediction of that trust, the grace of his grandmother and of his unlettered teacher. His grandmother slept at the foot of the hill, the banyan they planted over her must have grown into a big tree. Mohammed Haji too was gone.

'It is all over with the village,' Beeran said as he came to remove the coffee cup. 'The village died with the camp, and the school too was closed down. The tigers returned to our mountains, and the big spiders to the hilltop.'

Beeran withdrew with the tray, leaving Chandran alone. Chandran sat on in the verandah, and the sun climbed toward its zenith.

*

A few days after the incident of the wind flowers, Chandran composed a poem in English on butterflies. He had taken the first couplet from a book of nursery rhymes, but wrote out the rest himself. He showed it to his tutor.

'The first two lines are not mine,' Chandran confessed.

The tutor smiled, 'It does not matter.' He read through the poem and said, 'It is well done.'

Chandran took the poem to school and showed it to the headmaster. The headmaster read it out to the children of the eighth standard, the highest class in the school. When the poem was written out in the school's manuscript magazine, there were sceptical whispers. How could a boy of the fifth standard know so much English? Even Mohammed Haji could not have written that poem. Raghavan, the overgrown back-bencher, swore that Chandran's grandfather had written the poem.

It was then that another incident brought the children's resentment out into the open. Mohammed Haji was spelling out the word 'depot', and wondered aloud whether the final 't' was voiced or not. He came up to Chandran and said, 'You read.' Chandran read the word out, with the 't' silent. A murmur went through the class, and Khadija, the Muslim landlord's daughter, said, 'Why do you ask him?'

Mohammed Haji caressed Chandran's shoulders, and told Khadija, 'O child of the devil, isn't he the one who is learning English at home?'

The English lesson ended and Mohammed Haji, tapping the table with his cane for silence, announced the next lesson, 'Now all of you go down into the lane and chase butterflies. It is nature study till lunch-break.'

With shouts of joy the children tumbled out of the classroom.

'Anyone to the riverside?' Khadija called out. Hymavathi, Amina and Aisu joined her.

'Shall we go too?' Visalakshi asked Chandran.

'Yes.'

When they got to the river Khadija said to no one in particular, 'It is depott! The 't' is not silent. My brother told me.'

'What about the teacher then?' Hymavathi asked.

'All that is like the poem,' Khadija said.

Amina asked Chandran, 'Did you write it yourself?'

Chandran flushed. He said, 'Yes, I did.'

Amina feigned surprise, '*Ya Rahman*!'

Khadija, who was listening, said, 'A lie!'

Visalakshi lashed out, 'Didn't the headmaster read it out? Are you calling the headmaster a liar?'

That silenced Khadija.

'Chandran, let us go,' Visalakshi said. She led him back to school, and the other children who remained behind on the river bank dared not snigger. Walking up the lane between embankments of fern, Visalakshi paused. 'Chandran,' she said, 'don't be sad.'

At this Chandran's tears came rolling down.

'*Ayyee*!' she said, 'Why do you cry? I shall take you to the orchard and pluck you the *ambazha* fruit.'

'No.'

'Come along,' she said, grasping him by the shoulder. 'Don't you want to see the orchard?'

A narrow lane led to the orchard, and one had to cross a steep stile to get among the trees.

'Are you scared, Chandran?' Visalakshi asked, as she helped Chandran over the stile.

'No, Visalakshi. But aren't we getting late for class?'

'Don't worry.'

Chandran entered the enchanted grove, he had never been inside an orchard before. He looked up at the branches arched beneath the sky and listened to the tumult of the cicadas as they jingled their mysterious hoards of silver.

Visalakshi was familiar with the secrets of the orchard. 'Karinagattan lives here.'

'Who is that?'

'He is a god. The snake-god.'

'Will he bite?'

'I don't know. Perhaps, if we step on him. Are you scared?'

'No.' But Chandran was afraid not so much of snake bite as of his father coming to know of this expedition. He was the Commandant's son, and it was not proper for him to have gone into the orchard foraging for the wild *ambazha* fruit. If the snake-god bit him all his secrets would be out, the forays into the areca plantation, the journeys to the riverside. O' serpent-god, he prayed, help me keep my secrets.

Visalakshi plucked the *ambazhas* and gave them to him. Chandran bit into them. Some were sour, yet others bitter.

'Aren't they tasty?' Visalakshi asked.

'Yes.'

They were busy plucking fruits when the bell rang for re-assembly.

'Chandran!'

'Shall we run?'

'It is the geography teacher's class. He will cane us.'

They left the orchard and broke into a run. In the embarrassment of truancy they hesitated at the entrance to the classroom. The geography teacher turned from his map and asked them, 'Where have you been?'

Neither Visalakshi nor Chandran replied. But from the back bench an informer piped up, 'They were in the orchard, Sir.'

Chandran was terrified, for the orchard was forbidden territory. The cane lay on the table. The geography teacher regarded the delinquents in indecision for a while, and then said, 'Get in.'

That evening the car did not arrive to take Chandran home. Instead, an orderly waited with biscuits and a flask of milk. After he had eaten Chandran set out. He found Visalakshi waiting at the gate.

'Where is your car, Chandran?'

'My father has taken it. He is on tour.'

Chandran and Visalakshi walked behind the orderly.

She said to him softly, 'We escaped a caning because of you.'

The road to the camp climbed steeply. Midway was Visalakshi's house. This was where old Raman Nair ran his village hotel and place of entertainment. It had an austere look compared to other tea-shops. There was no glass front, no funnelled gramophone. Still soldiers frequented the place, and so did landlords from the deep countryside.

As they reached her house, Visalakshi said shyly, 'Will you come in, Chandran?'

He had dreamt of going into that charmed house every time he drove past it. He would see Raman Nair seated in the verandah, or at times catch a glimpse of Visalakshi's mother, her face fair and bright. Today he was at its very threshold. The temptation was irresistible. He would be late getting home, but could pacify his mother with some alibi. But there was the orderly, he would never consent to the visit. Taking a desperate chance, Chandran asked the orderly, 'Nambiar, can I go with her?'

Nambiar consented with unexpected readiness. In exuberant joy Visalakshi bolted in, crying, 'Mother! Look who has come!' Visalakshi's mother emerged from the kitchen through a smoky corridor. Her face was flushed with the fires of the hearth, and reddened a little more as she blew her nose. Chandran saw the drops of sweat under her lips, the patch of soot on her dimple and sensed her fragrance like Visalakshi's in the river breeze. Flashing a seductive smile at Nambiar, Janaki-amma turned to Chandran tenderly, 'We are honoured!'

Visalakshi insisted that he should have coffee. Chandran's confusion increased. This visit was in defiance of his parents' ban on fraternizing. He wondered if the orderly would turn informer. Presently Visalakshi returned with a tray of biscuits and coffee and said, 'Let us go into my room.' She led the way into a little room in the corner of which were stacked her worldly possessions: a sea shell, a bronze Krishna, a few marbles, a collection of copper and silver coins. Above this treasure hung a garlanded photograph.

'Whose picture is that?' Chandran asked.

'It is my father's.'

The reply struck Chandran as odd. 'Then,' he asked hesitantly, 'who is Raman Nair?'

'Aw,' she said. 'He keeps my mother.'

Her reply baffled him. He asked, 'Doesn't your father stay here?'

'He stays faraway, in Manjeri.'

Janaki-amma came in and stroked Chandran's cheeks. 'Have some biscuits, child. It is poor fare.'

'Oh, no,' Chandran said, and hastened to eat the biscuits which were stale and damp. Janaki-amma smiled as she watched him and the dimples deepened on her cheeks. As she smoothed back her curls her face was like Visalakshi's, so were her large, black eyes, her delicate feet, and the soft touch of her hands. Janaki-amma left the children and went away to entertain the orderly.

'Don't you like my mother?' Visalakshi asked.

'Yes.'

'Isn't she pretty?'

'She is.'

'Her thighs are very fair.'

'You have seen them, have you, Visalakshi?'

'Yes.' she said. 'Mother is very young, and Raman Nair is old. Mother says he is ninety.'

'And how old is your mother?'

'She is sixteen.'

'Is that true?'

'It is. All her visitors say so.'

Chandran ate the rest of the stale biscuits and hard bananas with relish.

'Why doesn't your father stay here?'

Visalakshi did not reply. Chandran asked again, 'Doesn't your father visit you, Visalakshi?'

A sadness misted her face, a sadness beyond Chandran's understanding.

Visalakshi said, 'He did come some time ago, when Raman Nair was away. It was sad seeing my father, he was so poor and worn. He works in a plantation in Manjeri, and they pay him scanty wages. Mother sat with him in her room, and they talked till evening, when he wanted to go away by the last bus. *Oh, no, don't*, mother said, *you don't love me*! She kept taunting him, and father agreed to stay the night. When mother went for her evening bath, father put me on his lap and told me, *you must study well, my child, and become a teacher in the big school at Manjeri*. He said he was saving from his wages so that I could go on with my schooling. He misses supper to save this money for me, and that has given him an ulcer. He said he will move on to larger estates in the mountains where they paid better wages. He is doing it all for me. That evening he wept over me, and said again, *you should become a teacher, my child. You should not become like your mother*. What did he mean, Chandran?'

'I don't know, Visalakshi.'

Visalakshi went on, 'That night I couldn't sleep. In my mother's room I could hear them whispering, and father repeating her name, sobbing, *Janu, Janu*! I pressed my face into the pillow and cried myself to sleep. When I woke up father was gone.'

When the story ended, Visalakshi was greatly depressed. She asked, 'Does your mother have another man, someone who keeps her?'

'No.'

Visalakshi fell silent for a while, then went over to her treasure trove. 'Chandran...'

'Yes?'

'Take a gift, Chandran. Anything you like.'

'Oh, no!'

'Aren't we friends?'

'Of course, we are.'

'Then choose your gift.'

She placed the bronze Krishna before him. It was her father's gift and she polished it every day with sour tamarind.

'Not that, Visalakshi,' Chandran said. 'That is too precious.'

Reluctantly she put the Krishna back. 'Then at least this sea-shell,' she said.

'If you insist.'

Chandran put the shell into his satchel. It was getting late.

'Visalakshi, I must go.'

It was the orderly that Chandran was anxious about, but Nambiar showed no sign of impatience. He sat in Janaki-amma's room, chatting with her, and bursting into peals of laughter. That reassured Chandran. Surely if the orderly was so friendly with Visalakshi's mother, he would not turn informer.

'What do they call you at home, Chandran?' Visalakshi asked.

'They call me Kunchu.'

'And me, they call Chinnu.'

The visit ended. That night Chandran tossed sleepless in bed for a long while. And when he slept, strange dreams came to him. He dreamt that he was Janaki-amma's child, a nurseling. Janaki-amma was only as big as Visalakshi, and had the same riverside fragrance. Yet she had large pale breasts with which she suckled him. He slept clutching those breasts with infant's hands.

*

Beeran waited in ill-tempered patience, Chandran had said he would be leaving after breakfast, yet he sat on. *Forgive me, Beeran. This is a wait I cannot help, a wait for noontide, for the river sands to become hot.*

*

The visit could not be kept a secret for long, the Commandant found out after a few days. The orderly was severely reprimanded and Chandran received another sermon on dignity, he was the Commandant's son, and ought to keep his distance from the village children. But, once in school, this oppressive dignity gave way to freedom.

'Kunchu, let us go!' Visalakshi would call at lunch-break.

'Let us,' he would say. They wandered in the neighbourhood during lunch-break, taking in the magical sights of the village. They watched old Muslims sit stooped, hollow goats' horns stuck on their shaven heads to let barber-surgeons draw out impure blood. Visalakshi taught Chandran to climb over the stile, and they foraged in the orchards. They hunted among ferns for cocoons, watched giant dragonflies plummet into the river and rise, and schools of tiny silvery fish churn in the deep eddies. Chandran often slipped on the riverside rocks of quartz with their cover of velvet moss, but Visalakshi, sure-footed, always held him. It was while watching the eddies once that Visalakshi narrated the story of how the Muslim rebels murdered the Namboodiri landlord and flung his body into the river.

'It was my father who shot the rebels,' Chandran said. He had seen his father wear a silver medal with King George's head embossed on it. His father had been decorated for suppressing the rebellion. Visalakshi's eyes widened in wonder. 'Is that so, Kunchu?'

'He shot them with a big gun. Have you seen a big gun, Chinnu?'

'How could I?'

'*Ayyee!* You haven't seen a Lewis gun? It has a magazine of forty-seven rounds, and can kill two thousand people. It was with the same gun that the leader of the rebellion was shot too. My father shot him.'

'Kunchu, will you take me to see this gun someday?

'Of course.'

It was in the days after the promise that Chandran was terrified by what he had let himself in for. How could he invite Janaki-amma's daughter home, what would he tell his father? It was then that an opportunity presented itself. The Commandant left on a tour of inspection and was expected to be away for a week. Chandran trailed his mother round the house, his heart beating fast.

'What is it, Kunchu?'

'Mother, this class-mate of mine...'

'What about your class-mate?'

'She wants to see the camp.'

'Why do you have to ask me?'

'She wants to see the Lewis gun.'

'Who is she?'

'Chinnu,' the word slipped out of his mouth.

'Chinnu who?'

Chandran's face reddened in confusion.

'Visalakshi, Raman Nair's daughter.'

Chandran's mother laughed. 'Why don't you wait till father returns?'

That would ruin everything, Chandran was on the verge of tears. Unexpectedly his mother said, 'Call her if you want to.'

The next evening Visalakshi came home with Chandran. Chandran's mother received her with effusive courtesy, but Chandran himself shied away.

'You ought to be chaperoning her, Kunchu,' grandmother chided him. 'Isn't she your friend?'

Mother was amused. 'Come, Kunchu, pass her the cake.'

After tea his mother called the orderly and said, 'Nambiar, could you take the children to see the guns?'

The gun-room was a narrow corridor dimly lit by high ventilators, its still air heavy with the smell of grease and oil. It held row upon row of rifles along with stacks of magazines and grenades, and laid out on cement racks, the heavy Lewis guns, sombre like the trunks of elephants.

'*Ayyo!*' said Visalakshi, holding her breath. Chandran felt a great tide of love rise within him and sweep over her.

'Are you scared, Chinnu?'

'*Ayyo!*'

She stood awhile in silence and asked him, 'Is that the big gun you father used?'

'Yes,' Chandran answered hastily. He was not sure, and did not want to risk talking about it in the presence of the gun-keeper.

'*Ayyo!*' Visalakshi repeated.

*

There were a number of factions in the class, led by Abu, by Salim, by the Muezzin's daughter Mariam, and so on. Each of these factions had tried to claim Chandran, but he had rebuffed them all, and consequently all of them turned against him. It did not matter, he would not condescend to belong to any faction. He was the Commandant's son after all. Despite the reclusive superior air he adopted, Khadija ventured to call him a liar a second time. Her uncle, who traded in Malaya, had brought home a silver inkpot. She brought it to class and proclaimed, 'There is no inkpot like this anywhere in the world.'

Chandran laughed. On his father's table was an identical piece.

'We have one at home,' he said.

'Oh, ho! Here is the one who has everything!'

'I shall bring it to school tomorrow.'

'Let us see you bring it!'

Chandran realized the predicament he was in. He dared not displace anything on the Commandant's table. When he came without the inkpot to school the next day Khadija shouted, 'Liar!' Chandran turned pale. If he wanted he could complain to the headmaster, but he reasoned himself out of such a course. More than the humiliation it was isolation that Chandran found hard to bear. No faction came to his rescue. In despair he glanced towards Chinnu. 'What is it all about, Khadija?' Visalakshi asked, pretending not to know. There was a titter in the class. Visalakshi said, 'Chandran didn't lie. I have seen the inkpot myself.'

God, she hadn't.

'How did you see it?' Khadija asked, the sparring now heady. 'Have you gone to his house?'

Embarrassed, Visalakshi admitted, 'Yes.'

'Ho, ho,' Khadija and her friends set up a chorus, 'ha, ha!'

Chandran and Visalakshi had kept the story of her visit a precious secret. It was now revealed before a leering, hostile class. An insensate courage seized Chandran. He would bring the inkpot, come what may. Let his father shoot him down with the Lewis gun, like he had shot the Muslim insurgents!

Chandran came to class the next day with the inkpot. Visalakshi did not bother to show her triumph. Khadija was silent. Hymavathi, Amina and Aisu turned away from the glittering object.

Then events took a disastrous turn. The inkpot slipped from his hand and fell and its engraved latch came off. Chandran despaired. Now his father would discover his transgression!

'We shall set it right, Kunchu,' Visalakshi said with confidence.

'How?'

'Just you wait.'

When the bell rang for lunch-break, Visalakshi led Chandran into the orchard. There was a tree in the orchard whose bark oozed an adhesive resin. It was called the *tholi* gum, and could mend practically anything. Visalakshi scraped off chunks of the resin and smeared it on the metal.

'Will it stick?'

'Of course.'

The gum made a mess on her palms, elbows and arms.

'Chinnu...'

'Yes?'

'The gum is all over you.'

'Where?'

'Here.'

'Where?'

Chandran wiped it away from her palms and from her elbows and arms. Traces of the resin lingered on her cheek. Tenderly, he began wiping it away.

'Is it going, Kunchu?'

*

God, if only it had ended there, this ballad of my love, with the ministering palm on the fair cheek! But it was destined for a grosser completion, by an intruding pimp.

'All that is left of this village,' Beeran said, 'is Raman Nair's hotel. The old man died, and after him his woman, getting rid of an inconvenient pregnancy.' Here Beeran paused and laughed, a pimp's idea of comic relief. 'Now the daughter reigns, and if she goes away that will be the end of this travellers' bungalow. She is worth her weight in gold.'

Chandran smiled in forgiveness, and rose. It was noon.

'Thank you, Beeran. I must go now.'

Dispiritedly Beeran helped with the boxes and stood by.

'*Salaam*,' he said.

'*Salaam*,' Chandran said.

The car sped down the hill and climbed up another. On either side of the road were mud walls with their veneer of moss and their mouldering smell. At the top of the hill, Chandran stopped his vehicle. This would be a brief tryst with the noontide. Were he to linger on he would disturb the slumbers of many. Of his grandmother who had invoked for him the benediction of an unlettered teacher, of the beautiful girl who had filled the river breeze with fragrance, of himself the child suckled by the pale breasts of innocence. *Let me leave all this undisturbed, let me resume my disconsolate journey.*

Far away, in the depths of another river, schools of fish churned with the eddies. Far away, on strange sands, in the heat of the noontide, in the grace of the preceptor, rose the splendrous wind flowers.

The Sleeping Valley

Forty students, soon to be Bachelors of Arts and Science, sat in the hall writing their final examination. I was invigilating. Perhaps it was the examination that brought back the memories, perhaps it was the muffled noise of the train hurtling through the valley far away.

My mind goes back fifteen years, to my unusual meeting with Mayuranadhan. I was a fresher. I was scanning the notice-board in the college to find out which room had been given to me in the hostel, when a big, noisy boy came up to me and asked, in a weird mixture of Malayalam and archaic Sanskrit, the number of my room. I told him it was 48.

'What a coincidence,' he said. 'So is mine. We share the room this year.' He shook my hand and introduced himself as the Lord of the Peacocks, which was an absurd English rendering of the Sanskritic roots of his name, Mayuranadhan. Then he asked me what subject I had chosen for my course. I told him it was history. Whereupon he said he had come to learn the science of the birds and the beasts. 'In common parlance,' he said, 'they call it zoology.'

I found his melodramatic manner intrusive, and was not amused. Besides, he had the swagger of the campus bully. I decided to keep my distance, though it was difficult, sharing a room as we did. Aside from his manner, I was wary of him on many counts. Mayuranadhan came from a wealthy family, and outraged me with his expensive habits, as also his neglect of lessons. I had left my village home and come here to the town to study, and was aware that I was causing my parents great hardship, which they bore in the hope that I would secure a degree and a job, and help them in their old age. They had cautioned me not to get mixed up with rich class-fellows — the wastrels and corrupters. My father wrote me long letters, often quoting from ancient ethical texts like *Todd's Students' Manual*. It was a curious turn of fate that had made me share a room with just the kind of boy they would have liked me to avoid.

In less than a month the hostel acknowledged Mayuranadhan as its principal tough. The swagger accounted for this in part, as did his physical growth which outstripped his real age. The pretty boys of the hostel were intimidated. So were the younger women instructors of the college, the swagger led them to believe he was making passes. Recalling the uneasy beginnings of my acquaintance with him, I marvel at the strange mantles people don, exteriors not of their choice or making. Before the first term ended I was beginning to discover the wayward little boy behind the theatrical and offensive facade.

Mayuranadhan skipped games in the evenings and took long walks into the enclaves of countryside in our college town. Soon he persuaded me to accompany him on his walks.

These walks invariably ended beside a disused pond full of hyacinth and water-lily. A railway line lay beside the pond, and all round were paddy flats. We would sit for a while on the pond's warm stucco embankment. Across the paddies was the old country house where Padmini, a class-mate of ours, lived. Padmini was much older than us, a widow with a son. Sitting on the embankment, as the afterglow of sunset died away, Mayuranadhan would take out scraps of paper and read out to me snatches of fitful love poetry, tributes to Padmini. These strange serenades seldom reached the object of their adoration.

A year went by, and we found ourselves sharing the same room after the summer recess. Mayuranadhan had got worse. He skipped classes or sitting in the back-benches for cover, read porn and pulp while the lectures went on. He never paid attention to his studies in the hostel room either. The nights, Mayuranadhan maintained, were for sleeping. That year he failed in both the mid-term examinations.

There was only a term to go for the finals. Mayuranadhan was unruffled. His anxious father wrote to him again and again, *How much have you revised? What grades do you think you will secure? Are you wasting time?* Mayuranadhan would wave the letters with a flourish and speak tender and grotesque nonsense, taking his father's name in irreverence, 'Look at this, room-mate! Poor dear Gopalan's anxiety! Hey, Gopalan! The Lord of the Peacocks will get through!' This ranting was usually followed by a noisy attempt to read, a wild collage of things from Wordsworth to the science of the birds and the beasts. In a quarter of an hour his enthusiasm would subside as also his guilt, and Mayuranadhan would bid me goodnight and get into bed. 'I am undone, room-mate!' The next morning he would be up barely in time to watch the rest of us in the hostel leave for our classes.

I reminded myself that Mayuranadhan did not need the education he was paying for, he came to it in an act of play. The two of us had come to college for different reasons, Mayuranadhan to satisfy a vicarious desire of his father, and I to qualify for a job. Mayuranadhan's father had not been able to afford college in his youth, but was now a wealthy builder, and could buy for his son anything that money could buy. And he pampered him with sumptuous allowances, which Mayuranadhan drank and whored away, almost with the ease of innocence.

Four days before the examination, as I sat with my books, Mayuranadhan wrote poetry. His usual mix of romance and doggerel. He smiled when I glanced at the sheet of paper. 'It is about Pappa my sweetheart,' he said. 'How do you like my verse of dedication?' Pappa was Padmini.

When I recall, after these years, the doggerel and the calf-love, I find myself ruefully speculating on what they might have flowered into in the fullness of time. But they were destined to become nothing, and perhaps Mayuranadhan strove for no other consummation.

This was not a night one could spend writing poetry, with so few days to go for the examination.

'How do you hope to write your papers?' I asked.

'You are a nitwit, room-mate! There are ways and ways...'

Mayuranadhan opened the drawer of his desk and took out rolled up paper ribbons on which were scribbled answers to a wide range of anticipated questions. He had duplicate sets, to insure against possible theft. No one stole them, and a day before the examination he sold the spare sets to fellow delinquents. As there were too many of paper rolls, an elaborate index was needed indicating where each roll was hidden away.

He wore an old watch, a keepsake with a broad leather strap. On the back of the strap he scribbled: *on the right hip, kites, falcons, owls. On the left hip, spiders, earthworms, snails...* 'It is my old age, room-mate,' he said. 'I am losing my memory.'

Both of us passed. Mayuranadhan had merely scraped through, and stayed back to do an ordinary Bachelor's programme in the old college. I moved to the city of Madras for my Honours. Mayuranadhan wrote to me frequently. Prolific and exuberant letters; reading them was like listening to his heady talk, his poetry and animated nonsense.

The examination came again, but the questions ranged wider. The paper rolls proved inadequate, so did the index on the strap of the old watch. Mayuranadhan failed, and failed again in the supplementary examinations. I did my Masters and became a college teacher. I was getting ready to go home for the Michaelmas break when I received Mayuranadhan's letter. He wanted me to visit his country home because, he said, he had taken a wife under unusual circumstances and wanted to talk to me about it. He wanted me to come whatever my other commitments.

*

It was an ancient house, the seat of an unpartitioned joint family, a house of magnificent pillars and arches; on the lands surrounding it grew rosewood and teak planted by bygone grandsires. Mayuranadhan had not finished his Bachelor's programme and still exulted in the melodrama of his paper rolls. He was overjoyed to see me. Seated in the portico, I waited impatiently to hear about his marriage.

Just then a middle-aged woman servant crossed the yard with a pitcher of water, her waist luxurious, breasts sagging, lips perpetually wet, with a compelling aura of nakedness.

'She is the one,' Mayuranadhan said.

I did not find it funny, it was feudal and depraved. For the first time in our long association Mayuranadhan realized that I was not seeing it the way he did, as a jest. He fell silent.

That evening Mayuranadhan took me to see his great-grandmother. She was ninety-four; and her grandchildren and great-grandchildren numbered over two hundred; this teeming multitude lived in houses spread over the neighbourhood, and came to the old family house for occasional reunions. The great-grandmother's memory had faded and her sight become enfeebled, and Mayuranadhan was just one among the dizzying numbers of her family. She called him Appu, which meant child, any one of the two hundred. She might well have counted me among the children but Mayuranadhan hastened to introduce me as his class-mate.

'What is that, Appu?' she asked.

'Well, it is like this: don't you remember the goddess of our temple?'

'Yes, the goddess, I remember.'

'The goddess and you took your lessons from the same *pandit*, didn't you, grandma?'

Grandma turned an antique smile on us. 'It was so long ago, Appu. My memory has grown foggy.'

'It is like that, grandma. This is Appu's friend, who takes lessons in law from the same judge as Appu does.'

Mayuranadhan spoke of himself in the third person in his usual theatrical manner. He went on: my father was an aircraft manufacturer whose hobby was pigeon racing. And I was a world famous tennis star.

'Don't you remember, grandma,' he said, 'how Appu and the white man played tennis once?'

Grandma began seeing it all again, a mortal duel in an ancient battle, dust rising from the combat. A *feringhee* tennis player named Arkinstall had once trespassed into Appu's college of law. Appu challenged him and trounced him in a game of singles. But Appu never told anyone about his victory.

'Why didn't you, Appu?' grandma asked.

'It is better to keep secrets. But this friend witnessed the game, he was the sole witness and umpire. I have told you all about it once before. Don't you remember, grandma?'

Grandma smiled again and said, 'Oh, yes, now I remember your friend.'

Grandma was curious, she wanted all the news of the outside world. 'Appu, my child, how goes the war?'

I was about to tell her that the war had been over ten years but Mayuranadhan pre-empted me, 'The war is on, grandma, it rages unabated.'

He fetched a scrap of newspaper and read out to her translating from the English into Malayalam. 'The fighting spreads. It is now over Raman Kutty Nair's estate! What damnation, grandma! The *feringhees* are all over old Raman Kutty Nair's farm.'

'Is that true, Appu?'

Mayauranadhan read on in English and translated, 'Hold on, grandma! All is not lost. The report goes on to say that the fighting has moved away.'

Grandma heaved a sigh. Mayuranadhan read on, 'Old Raman Kutty Nair is safe. But the *feringhees* have stolen a calf from his stables. The *feringhees* can't resist stealing.'

Grandma was agitated. 'Has the war really moved away, Appu?'

'It has, grandma.'

Grandma communed with her gods. 'Unseen ones, protect my children!'

I fancied Mayuranadhan complimented himself on his performance, an impresario's stagey self-approbation which I refused to countenance. In a letter he wrote to me later, he recalled this grim jest, 'You encounter death in the chamber of your ancestors, you mock it and come away. The grotesque epigram is completed.'

*

Time moved on, and some of us who had strolled through the corridors of the old college as wide-eyed freshers had become grown men, professionals, bureaucrats, politicians, traders. Living in big houses and driving around with winsome wives in gleaming automobiles. Yet others had been consigned to nondescript careers. They too had come to terms with their destinies and carried on.

'It is I who have come to terms with nothing,' Mayuranadhan wrote me, 'it is I who have stood still. Past my stillness Time moves on, yet Time must have a stop. Despite this knowledge, like Sisyphus, I wind my keepsake watch. What an instrument, room-mate! Inside it is the valley, the sunset, where all things sleep.'

After two years of teaching I went back to Madras to do research. Mayuranadhan corresponded less and less, until the letters stopped altogether. I was vaguely aware that he still had not obtained his Bachelor's degree. My research ended, I got ready to return to my home town. It was then one evening while taking a walk over the old fly-over at Egmore that I saw Mayuranadhan. It was like seeing an apparition.

'Don't be surprised, room-mate,' he said. 'I have been here these few months.'

He said he had come to the city to prepare for his examination through a tutorial institution in a last desperate bid.

'Did you know I was here?' I asked.

'I did,' Mayuranadhan said.

I felt repudiated and Mayuranadhan guilty; we walked on in oppressive silence to his apartment which was nearby.

It was a room in a ghetto off Hall's Road, the access to which lay through a common yard shared by a dozen tenements. In the middle of the yard was a tubewell, around which the women of the ghetto squabbled and slanged. Inside the room there were no longer the familiar scents of the colognes and the expensive cigarettes of my friend's earlier habitations. The room had a sense of indigence about it, the text books lay in a corner like debris, and on top of a rickety shelf stood a mounted photograph of Mayuranadhan's little brother.

I realized that the examination was to be held the next day, its proximity was ominous, repetitive. I hated to waste his time on so tense an evening. I rose to go.

'Stay, room-mate! There is so much to talk about.'

'Time is precious this evening.'

At the word *time* Mayuranadhan looked at his old keepsake watch. It had stopped. With a smile Mayuranadhan said, 'Time must have a stop!' I hated to let the conversation turn into those dismal channels, and so tried to distract him with a cigarette.

'Smells nice,' he said. 'Looks a classy cigarette. These days I am on *bidis*, the poor man's tobacco.'

Mayuranadhan began his story. Great-grandma was dead, and the property divided, and what had come to them was the remnants of the once prosperous estate. His father's building enterprise had got into deep trouble, the partners virtually at war with each other, and soon it was all over. His father had not pulled out in time, but had persisted petulantly and at great cost with the tottering enterprise. Another of his father's enterprises had been Mayuranadhan himself, whom the old man's fond obstinacy sent again and again to the examination hall.

'Enough of that,' Mayuranadhan said. 'Do you know what happened to Pappa?'

Padmini, heroine of Mayuranadhan's adolescent verse, had married a clerk in a transport company. A man from the Tamil districts bought the company. Padmini ended up as his mistress and moved with him to the Tamil country. Padmini's son had followed his mother over this cheerless trail, the years of his growing up haunted by the angst of Hamlet and Oedipus. At sixteen he committed a burglary.

'Poor dear Pappa!' Mayuranadhan said.

The twilight darkened. Around the tubewell the women jostled for water as in a primeval fight over mates, their skirts and wraps raised and tucked in at the waist, baring black thighs that seemed blacker in the twilight.

'Room-mate,' Mayuranadhan said, 'my wife is pregnant.'

'Your wife?'

'Yes, the woman I showed you.'

The distressing memory of it all came back to me. I found myself thinking of obscene solutions, cruelly practical. I asked him, 'Does she have a husband?'

'No alibi, if you are suggesting one. He has been dead these ten years.'

I thought of Mayuranadhan's father, the stricken patriarch stood defeated even on this, his last bastion. Mayuranadhan read my mind, 'It is over Gopalan that I grieve, room-mate. You do not know Gopalan. Very few people do. In his youth it was like Krishna's *Rasa Kreeda*—women, women, women! Yet he loved mother with a mad, mad love. He would croon to her and put her on his lap while we children watched aghast, and she herself melted away in embarrassment. Gopalan had no brains, but he loved like no man could, and repented as massively. The straightness of my path was his atonement.'

Mayuranadhan opened his briefcase. Inside it were those rolls of paper which had long ceased to be funny, and were now coils of sloppy tragedy. I pretended not to see them. Nor did Mayuranadhan draw my attention to them. He pulled out a letter, from his father, and gave it to me to read.

'Beloved Appu,' it read, 'you must try and pass this time. I need not remind you that now the burden of our family is on you. My stars failed me, there is no use turning back and regretting. If you endeavour, there is nothing we have lost which you cannot recover. My son, God has given you the gift of a healthy body and considerable talent. May he save you from distractions. Your little brother and sister live in the hope of your protection. Pray well and write. Good will befall you.'

His mother had added a few lines about the vow she had made to the family deity. And in a touching postscript was his little brother's demand for a hopping toy rabbit. In the script of children, spidery and uncertain, little Rajan repeated his request to make sure his brother did not forget.

Outside, the night of the ghetto grew heavy with the belligerence of people. Mayuranadhan smiled and said, 'What a jest, room-mate!'

*

After the summer recess, I went back to teaching. Mayuranadhan wrote me, 'Room-mate, in another month she will deliver. Well, so much for that.

'My rolls of paper were exposed. They have debarred me for three years.

'It was by an evening train that I left Madras. I hate to listen to trains whistling in the sunset.

'I had to hunt all over China Bazaar for the toy rabbit only to lose it in the train.

'Room-mate, do you remember the pond with water-lilies, and the railway line that goes past it, our unreal trysts? I revisited the place one evening. I sat beside the track, waiting for the rickety country train. It was then that the place gripped me with its sense of finality. The perfect locus for suicide.

'Oh, I forgot to tell you why I had gone there. Pappa is dead. Do you remember all that doggerel, silly and soulful, the indiscretions of growing up? I shall tell you a secret, it is incredible that I kept it all this while from you. We were in love...'

'Sir!'

I became aware once again of the forty examinees who sat before me, racing against time.

'Sir,' from a corner. 'Paper.'

I went over with the additional sheets, for a moment I stood taking in the ominous resemblance. A middle-aged examinee with sagging breasts, and, God, those nude, nude lips!

The examinees wrote on. In the next room someone wound a clock. The first bell rang, five minutes to go.

'Tie up your sheets!'

The rumble of another passing train. Over the palms of the valley its smoke was a fragile hem.

The letter continued: 'Never before have I felt this infirmity, the need to be seen as something other than the riotous me, the need to be understood by at least one person, a single person in the universe. Room-mate, you are my Horatio. If ever you pass that pond again, stay awhile in memory of me. Do not tread on those rails. Farewell, brother! My time stops, the enchanted valley calls me.'

Amid the palms the whistle of the train died away. The last bell rang.

'Stop writing!'

*

Time ends. There is no examination tomorrow. The examinees troop out, the scorers and the losers and the suicides. The hall is soon deserted.

I stand before the heaps of answer books, the scribbled testament of diverse hands. I wonder whether the flesh hurts as the wheels of the train run over it. Perhaps not, the train moves very quickly, giving little time for the awareness of pain. The red stains on the rails soon grow black and quiet. The rails, racing parallels, meet in the magical perspective of sunset. Beyond that is stillness, sanctuary. A gentle breeze blows around me from that far valley.

Pedal Machine

In the village of Playini near Palghat there lived a peasant couple, Nanjan and Neeli. They were not beautiful people, but to them was born a baby son of extraordinary beauty. They named him Pangi. As Pangi grew, his complexion became a vibrant fawn and his cheeks dimpled, but his shoulders and hips lacked all masculinity. Neeli died when Pangi was still a boy, and his father, who spent his days on the mountain sawing felled trees, found little time to raise him. Pangi dropped out of the village school where they taught the alphabet, writing on sand with the dried rind of wild fruit, and spent his time with the older pederasts of the village. He watched them at cards under the trees, and picked up the intricacies of the game, as well as snatches of obscene doggerel which he recited for their edification.

At this time a young and handsome German evangelist came to Playini. Those were the days of evangelist Gundert's dictionary, the first in the Malayalam language, and of itinerant Germans disseminating the Gospel in the native tongue. The listeners were aghast, because the language was that of the dictionary, and the periods came through in heavy Teutonic constructs. They met the Gospel with heathen laughter, and laughed for days after the evangelists had gone. The evangelist who came to Playini also spoke in the manner of his compatriots. He set up a wayside pulpit where a temple carnival was on and began addressing his listeners as sinners. Someone from the audience shouted, 'He calls us sinners. What have we done?' Thereupon, the oracle of the temple came out in a frenzy, smiting his own head with a sword. The white man abandoned his pulpit and fled. The villagers did not notice the young boy who followed the fleeing divine at a discreet distance.

Engelhardt, the priest, adopted the boy, and instructed him in the new native language of the Teutonic constructs, and the angular alphabet of the English Collector. Thus Pangi grew up, instructed and civilized and prettier than ever. Ten years went by, in prettiness and in the adoration of the Lord. When the dimples in his cheeks filled out, and the saplings they had planted in front of their bungalow became full grown trees, Pangi knew it was time to leave.

*

Early one morning the villagers of Playini saw a man riding a pair of wheels, crossing the pastures that lay beyond the village. Although he still had the traditional length of unsewn cloth round his waist, he wore a coat of blue serge that marked him out as a partial alien. The village women, sitting in the open grassland to defecate, rose hurriedly and lowered their clothing, and stood at ease over their little heaps of excrement. The rider moved past them, and announced his coming to the villagers. 'Catch me!' he cried. Soon a little crowd had gathered, and the strange two-wheeled vehicle plunged towards it, the rider shouting, 'Catch me!' Those were the early decades of Queen Victoria, and none of the villagers had seen a vehicle borne on two wheels; the bicycle was yet to make its appearance on the mud tracks of the countryside. The rider wanted the people to hold his machine so that its speed could be retarded and he could clamber down, but they would not touch it, fearing its metal to be irradiated with magnetic currents. The rider was desperate. 'There's nothing to fear,' he assured them. 'Just hold it.'

At last some of the crowd came forward to catch hold of the vehicle by its gleaming handlebars. The two-wheeled craft came to a halt, and the rider descended from the saddle with elaborate effort.

Narayana Tharakan, the owner of Playini's little tea-shop, peered out to greet the visitor. A visitor was a rare occurrence in Playini, this one was stranger than most, because he wore a coat of blue serge. The rider asked with the curiosity of an alien, 'Isn't that the village tea-shop?' Narayana Tharakan could not have heard the rider, who was yet some distance away, but he greeted him with the hospitality of the village, 'Come, come. This is a humble shop.' Part of the crowd followed the rider as he rolled the craft towards the tea-shop, in the manner of a man leading a horse. Athramkannu and Koru and old Chippu-achchan, the ones who had brought the craft to a stop, walked close behind the rider, who now leaned the craft against a tamarind tree. Looking up at the plentiful fruit, he asked again with the curiosity of an alien, 'Is it sweet or sour?'

'It's the tamarind,' old Chippu-achchan said, 'it's sour. The yield is good this year.'

A few children and women joined the crowd now, but old Chippu-achchan waved the children away; it was improper for a guest so distinguished to be beset by urchins.

The rider entered the tea-shop and sat. The crowd spilled into the little shop. Narayana Tharakan mixed a single cup of tea and poured it back and forth ceremoniously; the rider waved his hand to encompass the crowd and invited them all to a cup of tea. But the crowd would not move, nor would the shopkeeper pour out a second cup. The rider now insisted, 'At least our elder should drink with me.'

Narayana Tharakan looked from the rider to old Chippu-achchan and back again, with the anxiety of an investor. 'Shall I pour out another cup?' he asked.

'Please do,' the rider said.

'Well, well,' old Chippu-achchan said. 'I'll have the tea, since you all insist.'

The crowd would not leave. They were not interested in the tea, but were extremely anxious to know where the visitor had come from riding his strange craft. The visitor rose after he had drunk his tea, and took out a silver rupee from his pocket. The two teas cost four coppers, and the shopkeeper had to return fifteen annas and eight coppers to him. Narayana Tharakan did not have that much money. He looked around helplessly.

'Would you be having change, O Athramkannu?' Narayana Tharakan enquired without much hope. With a matching lack of enthusiasm, Athramkannu dipped his hands into the pouches of his broad green cloth belt and said, 'I think I am short by just a few coppers.'

Narayana Tharakan leaned out of the shop and called to the woman who kept shop two houses away, 'O Chettichiyar, would you be having change for a rupee?' The woman called back, 'I am sorry I'm short by a few coppers.'

The visitor gazed intently at the woman and asked, 'Isn't she the woman of the Chetty Oracle?'

'Of course, of course,' the astounded crowd answered.

'Did you know the Chetty Oracle?' old Chippu-achchan asked.

'Mmmm,' the visitor said mysteriously.

Narayana Tharakan came back uneasily to the question of the

fifteen annas and eight coppers. One would have to cross the fields and trek all the way to the farmhouse of the landlord to get that much change.

The visitor smiled. 'Please don't worry about the change,' he said lightly. 'It's no serious matter. And in any case, I can collect it later, because I'm going to be around.'

At this the crowd's curiosity turned almost hysterical. What did the stranger mean by saying he would be around? With a silly and embarrassed grin, preface to a tentative enquiry, old Chippu-achchan the village elder asked, 'Who might you be, visitor?'

The visitor was in no hurry to reveal his identity. Old Chippu-achchan drew closer and asked again, 'Might you be in the *poleeze* ?'

The rider of the two-wheeled craft made the sign of the cross. 'No,' he said, 'I do the work of our Lord and Saviour.'

The crowd was stunned into silence. The rider moved among them, scanning each face. 'Haven't you made me out?' he said. 'I'm Pangi, the son of Nanjan.'

*

Pangi stood a long while in silence in front of the old family home, holding his two-wheeled craft, and the crowd waited behind him. The little patch of ground was overgrown with wild plants, the hut was no more; Pangi did not attempt to trace its foundation beneath the wild growth, it was more consoling to watch the exuberance of the red spotted caladium. Nanjan had died when a tree crashed on him on the mountain five years ago, and old Theyyandi-achchan, his nearest relative, had looked after the house half-heartedly for some time. The kinsman drew close to Pangi and explained guiltily, 'Two years ago there was a big storm and it was too much for the old house.' Pangi was not listening; before him was the plentiful spread of the red spotted caladium. He was once again back in his childhood, when he had dug out the slender tubers, and his older friends had adorned him with caladium stems strung into grotesque garlands. Theyyandi-achchan broke Pangi's reverie; taking Pangi's hand, he said, 'Come, my boy. Let's go home.'

Together they walked to Theyyandi-achchan's house. The

crowd lingered outside the gate of bamboo. Theyyandi-achchan had already alerted his wife and seven daughters to the visitor's arrival and they squatted on the outer plinth of the hut. As Pangi crossed the yard they began a funeral lament for the woodcutter who had died five years ago.

'Ha, ha! You're not there to see it, father!

'Ha, ha, ha!'

A stray cat had chased a squirrel up into the top branches of a tamarind tree, and struggling to climb down, was moaning in fear. The old woman and her seven daughters, their eyes riveted on the cat, improvised further lines of the lament:

'Ha, ha, the son has come wearing the blue coat ha, ha!

'Who's there to see it, ha, ha, ha?

'The son has come riding the two wheels.

'You're not there to see it, father.

'You're not there ha, ha, ha!'

Pangi stood erect before the mourners, and made the sign of the cross. He spoke his native tongue with strange Teutonic resonance, 'It's all the Will of the Lord. Like our creditors who write off our debts, let us write off their sins. Amen!'

At this incantation, all life drained out of the mourners in the abrupt quiet that comes before a hysterical breakdown. The *ha, ha's* grew frantic, the women covered their faces with their upper clothes, and inside that privacy, the lament turned to wild heathen laughter. Its demoniac violence eventually wore them down, and they began to cry.

That night after a few drinks at the liquor-shop, Pangi wandered towards the burial marsh. Somewhere beneath its sodden earth, Nanjan slept. Beyond was the mountain pass. Pangi gazed at the moonlit silhouette of the Southern Ranges. The mountains brooded out there, quiet as a picture, but it was on their slopes that a wild tree visited his father with thunderous death. Ten years ago, when Pangi had followed the Teuton conqueror, his father was somewhere up there, finding his way through tangles of cane creepers. After the strenuous descent from the mountain he must have looked for his missing son throughout the village. And on the many nights that Engelhardt had sat in the moonlit garden caressing Pangi's dimples, his father must have walked again and again the tracks of the village, lantern in hand, in futile and insistent search. The moon set, and the mountain ranges were lost in the darkness. Pangi sat on a boulder, taking in the fragrance of the death mould. He sat there a long while, and when he came out of his reverie, the morning star had risen.

The following day was the day of the feast; it was both a funeral repast and a meal of homecoming. Theyyandi-achchan presented a sumptuous spread: salted fish, rice and sweetened pulses. The ritual mourning, which should have gone on for a fortnight, was confined to a day in view of the passage of time.

In reality, it was not the storm that had destroyed Nanjan's hut; soon after his death Theyyandi-achchan had stripped the hut of its woodwork and used it to build another living room in his own house. The rafters he had stolen had been tinted by tribesmen of the mountain, with secret vegetable and mineral pigments. Nanjan had carried them down to the plains on his shoulders.

While they waited for Pangi to arrive, the old woman and her daughters looked up at the rafters in great anxiety. 'O, god!' they whispered among themselves. 'Will he recognize the tints?' Well, if he did, decided the old woman, she would get him married to one of her robust daughters. Later as they sat down to feast, Theyyandi-achchan too looked up guiltily at the rafters, but worked up a reckless courage, and began chattering away.

'What is the custom of the whites, my child,' he began, 'is there a drink before the food?'

'Such is the custom,' Pangi said.

Theyyandi-achchan took out a bottle of fine distilled spirit. 'This may not match what you get from beyond the seas,' he said. 'This is made in our village.'

Pangi sipped the drink that was poured out for him with the tolerance of an alien.

'And my child,' Theyyandi-achchan went on, 'when is the walk? After the drink or after the feed?'(The native always spoke deferentially of the white man's meal as the feed). And every native knew that all white men had the ritual walk, the English Collector with his pedigree dog, even the German evangelist.

'Sometimes after the feed,' Pangi said, 'sometimes before.'

Huddled together at the far end of the room the old woman and her daughters were murmuring among themselves. 'What says my dear aunt?' Pangi asked.

'Ah, my child,' she said, 'we were talking about the tail.'

'The tail?' Pangi asked.

'Your aunt is talking about the white people,' Theyyandi-achchan said. 'Have you seen it, my child?'

'Seen what?'

'The tail.'

Pangi broke into shrill giggling. 'What ignorance is this!' he said.

The others looked at him in disbelief. The white man had a pink face, like Gauranga the monkey god, and it was but a reasonable supposition that he must have a tail hidden within his tubular apparel.

'It is possible you might never have seen it,' Theyyandi-achchan said. 'You might never have seen the white one without his clothes.'

Pangi almost answered that he had seen the whole of the white body, but hastily swallowed his words in distaste.

'If not a whole length, at least a rudiment,' Theyyandi-achchan persisted. 'This is true, say the wise ones, of the purer breeds of white man, like the Governor *Sahib*.'

The bottle was almost empty. The old woman pulled out a yard of smoked goat's gut, and roasted it over the cinders.

'Now, my son,' she said, serving the appetizing meat, 'I propose to ask you something which you should not take amiss. Have you accepted the Book of the white man?'

Pangi made the sign of the cross and answered, 'I'm with the undying God and the undying Truth.'

The Teutonic inflection had momentarily returned to his speech as he said this, causing the usual consternation among the listeners. The old woman chewed chunks of salted fish with frenetic concentration; she would not give respite to her teeth and lips, for fear the heathen laughter would come back to her. Theyyandi-achchan appeared calm, as though he had deep understanding of the undying God and the undying Truth.

'When you follow the Book,' he said, 'don't they give you a new name as well?'

'Patrose,' Pangi said. 'But to you I shall still be Pangi.'

'What's wrong with Patrose?' asked Theyyandi-achchan, 'Patrose, it's a nice name after all. Let it be.'

Theyyandi-achchan hoped that by supporting Pangi in everything, he could prevent him from identifying the provenance of the tinted rafters overhead.

The feast was over. Theyyandi-achchan invited Pangi to stay with them but he declined and left.

*

Pangi had a foster mother in Playini—Kalyani-achchi. She was a widow now, with a daughter Pangi's age, Devi. After Devi she lost two sons, and that was how she had come to mother Pangi in his vagabond childhood... The day after the feast Pangi visited Kalyani-achchi.

'I knew you had come back, son,' she said.

Memories came flooding in, memories of her motherhood and his wanderings. Kalyani-achchi had not changed much in the ten years he had been gone, except to acquire the handsome heaviness of middle age, the streaks of grey along her temples endowing her face with a new vivacity. They had much to say to each other. Of Nanjan's death, the terrible bolt of lightning which had killed Kalyani-achchi's husband, and how Theyyandi-achchan had robbed the tinted rafters. They talked from afternoon to sundown, then Devi lit the oil lamp and sat back listening.

'Do you remember, my son,' Kalyani-achchi asked, 'how I made you palm sugar tackies?'

'I remember, Kalyani Ma.'

'Do you remember your great fever?'

'I remember, Ma.'

'And how you were chased by the rabid dog?'

'I do.'

What memories, Devi wondered, and smiled to herself in tender jealousy; this was after all her mother's male child! The reminiscences grew into the night, and in the magic garden of motherhood flowered the red spotted caladium... Kalyani-achchi readied a corridor as Pangi's living room. In all this time she had only Devi, her daughter, for company, just the two of them, women; Pangi would give them some security.

Towards the end of their conversation Kalyani-achchi enquired of Pangi, out of concern for his well-being, 'Shouldn't you be working, my son?'

'But I am,' Pangi answered.

The words had come out despite himself, and now they committed him desperately to invent a whole enterprise.

'I'm in the insurance business,' Pangi said, investing the fantasy with precise and picturesque details. This was a company, from beyond the seas naturally, and it had an establishment in the mountain town of Simla. It insured cattle, and gave him a salary and allowance. The managers had even promised him a share in the profits.

'So, you'll move into town to work?' she asked.

Again, the desperate inventiveness. Pangi said, 'I'm got going anywhere. My principals want me to open an office in Playini.'

Kalyani-achchi wished him well. In a few days Pangi was at work, right in Kalyani-achchi's corridors. He hung up a thin plank of wood on the tamarind tree in front of the house, on which was drawn the head of a buffalo with lime, turmeric and coal. Below the head was written in unsure characters: *The Simla Company for cattle. Cash on the death of the animal. Insure! Insure*! Nobody in Playini could read, nevertheless, they trusted writing as the law.

Playini christened the two-wheeled craft 'The pedal machine'. And though he wore the unsewn cloth round the waist that all the villagers wore, unlike them Pangi did not go shirtless or barefoot. He always had his blue serge coat on, and on his feet were shoes fastened with laces. Thus he appeared every morning, part villager, part Teuton, part heathen and part evangelist, with his symbol of the power beyond the seas, the pedal machine. Unfortunately Pangi had not mastered the art of mounting and dismounting; he needed people to put him on the saddle, to stop the craft at its destination and help him dismount. The people of Playini had only heard of pedal machines until Pangi came to the village; it was said that there were five of them in the town of Palghat, four in the possession of white men, and the fifth with a princeling. Only the white men could mount and dismount on their own; the princeling, like Pangi, needed help. He kept his bicycle along with his elephants in the stable, and smeared its joints with *ksheerabala*, an expensive unction used for rheumatoid illnesses in humans.

The people of Palghat town were aware of the greater mastery the whites had over their pedal machines. 'The white man is the ocean crosser and the conqueror,' they said, with the deep dejection of a subjugated race. Yet they found some recompense in the fact that, after all, there were things the white man could not do. He could not, for instance, tap toddy, he could not ride the black palm into the bejewelled thunderstorms, and he could not fondle his women with the callused hands of the palm climber.

Now, despite his own partial identification with the Teuton, Pangi decided to vie with the white ocean crosser. Accordingly, every morning, on the village pasture where the women defecated, Pangi ran with the pedal machine and tried to mount it with one leg thrown over the saddle from behind. Each time the pedal machine and rider came tumbling onto the grass. While the pedal machine escaped lightly from these falls, as it was padded with rags and straw, Pangi himself was sorely bruised.

At the end of many days of such futile attempts, Chippuachchan, the village elder counselled Pangi, 'Why do you despair thus, my son? Aren't we all here to help?' Reluctantly Pangi agreed. And so began a period of peace with the pedal machine. When Pangi was ready, four or five young men would hold the machine for him, and he would mount it with the ceremony of a prince mounting his elephant. Once firmly in the saddle, Pangi would give the signal for the push. 'Push on!' the villagers would respond and with four or five men pushing, and another ten at some distance experiencing vicarious excitement, and often the village dogs providing full throated cacophony — the little procession would move some distance until the pedal machine's gyroscope stabilized, and Pangi took off.

Those were times when there was no traffic on the mud roads and Pangi would sail on with the wind, the wind which blew down the mountain pass with the aromas of the forest. He could cruise up to the village of Puthupiriyaram eight miles away and, if the wind was strong enough, even upto Mankara, eighteen miles distant. Whichever was the port of call, he would shout out from a distance, assuring the villagers that there were no magnetic currents in his machine. During these expeditions Pangi noticed that it was the Hindu villagers who were hesitant to touch the machine. The Muslims had no such fear. The white men mounted and dismounted with ease, and the Muslims had no dread of magnetic currents.

As days went by Pangi became obsessed with the facility of the white men; why did they find it so easy, when he and the native princeling found it so much trouble? He soon became enwrapped in the theology of the difference. And the longer he pondered the more convinced he became that the white man's and the Muslim's strength came from their Semitic religions. True, he had become Patrose, but he had not known faith, he had merely given himself up to a handsome Teutonic evangelist.

And so it was, as he coasted down the mud roads like a sloop in the east wind, he was filled with the agony for a new revelation.

One midnight the residents of Playini woke up to the noise of a hundred crackers. It came from the direction of Kalyani-achchi's house. The people rushed there. In the little yard of the house, beneath the tamarind tree, a wooden cross had been planted. Dressed in his coat of blue serge, Pangi sat before the cross. Round his neck were garlands made of *thechi* flowers. His hands were drenched with the blood of slaughtered chickens, sacrificial offerings, and he brandished the sword of the oracle.

*

The next morning Pangi rolled out his pedal machine. The villagers came to help as was their usual practice, but Pangi told them to stand aside. He ran with the pedal machine a hundred yards and tried to mount it with a leg thrown over the saddle. The front wheel took an acute turn, and both craft and rider fell to the ground. Blood stained his unsewn cloth. In a rage Pangi pulled off the cloth and, twisting it, tied it round his waist—a girdle over the blue coat.

The previous night, in a decision to cast away the vestiges of heathenism, he had abandoned the traditional loin cloth. Now, as he picked up the pedal machine, his nakedness showed beneath his coat. Pangi returned to the starting point and got ready for the second run; he cried out aloud, 'On earth as it is in the clouds!' His rage mounting, he ran forward with the pedal machine. Now, in biblical response there came a gust of wind, and the dust rose like a sea amid the black palms. Terrified, the people saw him riding through the dust half a mile away; they were witnesses to a miracle. Finally they heard his thundering cry, 'Amen!'

*

Pangi had been in Playini three months. One day a clasp came loose from the bicycle. Devi and Kalyani-achchi were greatly saddened. The mother decided that it was the evil eye; to exorcise it, she burnt incense before the machine. Pangi consoled her, and soon the machine was bodily carried to the town of Palghat. It was carried back a week later, its injury healed.

But Kalyani-achchi was not easily pacified; not only did she burn incense before the pedal machine, she burnt incense before the coat of blue serge and the shoes as well. These were things from across the seas, they could just as easily attract the evil eye. It was rumoured in Playini that the white man had willed many more things to Pangi, a matter which Pangi neither affirmed nor denied.

Even though three months had passed Pangi's enterprise had not begun in earnest. On the tamarind tree and along the hedge Pangi had hung up thirteen more pictures of buffalo heads until he was seized with an urge to draw even more. This he did like a prophet translating his vision into graffiti. Of an evening one might find Pangi on the outskirts of the village, scrawling on rock with an iron stylus. The next day he would be doing it elsewhere. The village was overwhelmed with a pantheon of buffalo heads which stared down at them from tree and rock. At last Mannadiar, the landlord, called on Pangi. 'How far have you got with the insurance?' he enquired.

'Everything is going according to plan,' said Pangi.

Mannadiar did not insure any cattle during this visit and Pangi did not press him. But Mannadiar repeated the visits; he had secret plans of persuading Pangi back into the native faith, and he decided to spread his persuasion over a number of visits. But each visit spurred Pangi on to fantasize until he had so filled Mannadiar with a glittering vision of the enterprise across the seas that the landlord could resist no longer.

'I shall bring my cows and buffaloes,' Mannadiar offered.

Pangi played hard to get. 'You've to wait a little longer,' he said. 'The forms should come from across the seas, the printed forms.' The long wait wore Mannadiar down, and after the harvest he visited Pangi, and asked in exasperation, 'When are the papers coming?'

Pangi answered him coolly, 'They've come.'

Mannadiar had his four buffaloes and a hybrid cow insured. In a spirit of generosity he paid for insuring the ownerless sacred bull of the village as well. With this Pangi's enterprise became credible to the villagers. If the landlord could trust Pangi, who couldn't? Twenty more scrawny beasts of the village passed under insurance cover. Soon villagers from far away led their animals to Playini. Most mornings saw herds of black buffaloes waiting at Kalyani-achchi's gate, full of drowsy unconcern for personal survival.

'The boy's stars are bright,' the people of Playini began saying.

'What doubt is there? He travels on the pedal machine like the princeling of Kollengode.'

'He doles out the white man's currency.'

'And they've promised him a share in the profits!'

The girls of the village and their parents began taking Pangi seriously. Theyyandi-achchan had seven daughters, three of the elder girls ripe for marriage, but Pangi's relations with them had cooled off; Theyyandi-achchan suspected it was the tinted rafters. Perhaps Pangi was planning to settle down with Devi; Devi had once been married for half a year to a man who went mad. Even this was a blemish in the village, but Kalyani-achchi had mothered Pangi and so, the gossip went, he would repay that love by succouring the girl. Kalyani-achchi herself was a beautiful woman, but out of concern for her daughter, she had turned down marriage proposals from widowers and old bachelors. She had lived solely for her daughter and perhaps all those years of sacrifice were now going to be recompensed.

*

The enterprise was now a year old, and it had grown immensely. A former tout from the town's cattle fair, a boy named Kotharami, joined Pangi as his principal executive. Independent touts too flourished around the enterprise, and Narayana Tharakan sold more *vadas* and tea as cattle owners from other villages visited Playini. He even improvised a quick trade in cattle feed. Soon it was a great rush of cattle, and occasionally Pangi turned down an animal on grounds of health. Pangi himself was the medical examiner; the owner held the animal by its horns and Kotharami by its hind legs. With the animal thus secured, Pangi tapped its belly with a gavel, then thrust ground chillies into its nostrils to make it bellow. In a few cases he examined the eyes and ears through a glass prised out of an old pair of spectacles. Not many animals were rejected, but the owners of the rejected animals came back to Pangi, trying to influence him with recommendations. Pangi threatened them with the white man's law and they went back to their villages, humiliated and sad.

With the growth of business, Pangi had his first taste of riches and soon began lusting for more. He offered incentives to the touts and to the owners. For those who brought in three animals in one lot he offered a half chicken as bonus, for four animals a chicken and a quart of spirit; thus were the incentives graded up to a duck and a bottle of spirit, and so on. He had these incentives tom-tommed about by the village cobbler. The incentives worked, and the rush of money made Pangi heady. From incentives he moved on to intimidation—the cattle owners, he decided, should be threatened with impending catastrophe. He sat in the tea-shop and embarked on a gruesome fantasy. 'Sign up quickly,' he said. 'They say a cattle disease is coming.'

The fantasy soon grew explicit in its details: in the eastern districts, beyond the mountain pass of Palghat, an epidemic was poised to cross the frontiers. Pangi was both narrator and listener, and, as the story rolled out of the caverns of his mind, he found himself listening in virgin dread. Pangi wanted to halt its flow, but could not. The mesmeric tides thundered all round him while the buffaloes, their black heads swollen, cried out in mortal pain. Cows' guts slithered out like red spotted pythons. The crystal eyeballs of the calves flew away as beetles. Pangi had no respite. The epidemic surrounded him, a giant astral halo.

A few days later, wearing the halo, Pangi came to Narayana Tharakan's tea-shop and settled down to resume the epic. But as he began, Playini's blacksmith interrupted, 'In Pallanchathanur a kinsman of mine lost a pair of bulls last week.'

'Were they stolen?' Pangi asked in alarm.

'No. They died of the epidemic.'

Pallanchathanur was a nearby village; the halo had suddenly become a punitive Saturnian ring.

Now Athramkannu volunteered another piece of information, almost nonchalantly, 'Pallivela-achchan's young buffalo has a swelling in its head.'

'Is that true?' Pangi asked.

'What else is it but the truth? His little girl herself told me.'

The halo disintegrated and vanished, and Pangi rose without it and made his way home...

*

Pangi sat slouching on Kalyani-achchi's verandah. Kalyani-achchi peeped out from the door and said, 'Aren't you coming to eat?'

'I've no appetite.'

Pangi withdrew to the corridor and lay down. In a corner was a stack of printed paper on which men and cattle set their covenant. It thwarted sleep. He thought of walking up to Pallivela-achchan's cattle-shed, but the next instant decided against it. In that cattle shed was death. Pangi withdrew into the ignominious privacy of his mind, the mind which had a little while ago created the great optimism of death, and there fell into absurd meditation. Through the meditation, across its stretch of gravel and clod, with the insistence of a metronome, came the clip-clop of buffalo hooves. It was Pallivela-achchan's black buffalo, coming to the tryst of truth.

Pangi lay thus in the corridor the whole day; he neither ate nor drank. That night neither mother nor daughter slept. Hours before sunrise Pangi woke to his own dawn of terror, and lay wide-eyed on his mat. The noises of the dawn outside sounded harsh. As Pangi tried to sleep again, there was an insistent call at the gate, 'Pangi! Pangi!'

Pangi tried to shut out the call but could not. He rose, drowsy, and walked to the gate, drawn by the droning, insistent call. Pallivela-achchan stood at the gate. Pangi knew what the man had to say.

'My buffalo is dead,' Pallivela-achchan announced cheerfully.

The Patrose inside Pangi set to work. Patrose said, 'All right, go home and get the papers.'

Pangi was not without a faint hope that the papers might be misplaced or even lost, but the owner of the buffalo, taking care of every eventuality, had secured the papers in a length of hollow bamboo.

'As you say,' Pallivela-achchan said. 'I shall go and get them.'

Patrose continued, 'There are more things to be done, a lot more. The company's Inspector has to come and the picture of the carcass taken with the picture box. Better keep it safe.'

Pangi mounted his pedal machine and set off to Palghat town. He returned late evening. He told Pallivela-achchan that the Inspector and the man with the picture box would be there any time. It was Wednesday. Pallivela-achchan waited till Saturday. Saturday evening Pangi admitted that the functionaries were unlikely to come on a Sunday. He spoke to the villagers on the importance of the Sabbath. But no Sabbath was strong enough to restrain the buffalo's carcass. It began to stink. As the people perched on the culvert and on the branches of the banyan tree in eager expectation of the Inspector's arrival, the stench seeped through Playini like retribution.

It was Monday. A cluster of people stood before Kalyani-achchi's gate; the Inspector would come, they had decided, today. But when, even at noon, there was no sign of the Inspector, they began to get restless. At sundown Pallivela-achchan and a few villagers waylaid Kotharami in front of the liquor shop. 'Where is that bastard, your Inspector?' they demanded.

Kotharami was outraged by this irreverence to things from beyond the seas; he pitied the small concerns of the village. 'The Inspector cannot be dancing round your buffaloes,' he rasped. 'He has a hundred things to do, and much more important.'

'But by then Brother Buffalo will go his way,' someone from the crowd said.

In the crowd were the Chakkiliyas, the outcast community of cobblers who lived outside the village, and were the traditional scavengers of carcasses. They bought the dead animals and used both meat and hide. Even if the meat was partially putrid, they would salt it, and dry it in the sun, the mild taint acting as spice. The hide was cured into leather. If, however, the carcass rotted altogether, it would become useless. But the laws of the white man were relentless and no matter how long it took for the Inspector to arrive, the buffalo would have to lie in state.

The next day too the Inspector did not show, but Pangi

agreed, as a good villager, to mitigate the rigour of the white man's law. He produced a printed form on which he made Pallivela-achchan affix his thumb impression against half a dozen columns. 'I should not be doing this,' Pangi said, 'but after all, there are the bonds of the village, and I must share your troubles. I'm taking a big risk. Sell the meat, but keep the hide, and the head and horns. That will be the security for your money.' Pallivela-achchan was thankful for this small mercy. The Chakkiliyas trooped in like the dark servitors of Yama the Death God, and began hacking the carcass open. But Pangi demanded that they too should affix their thumb impressions to the paper because it was so enjoined by the white man's law. The outcasts had never touched paper in their lives and were overcome by dread. It took a lot of persuasion before three of them finally pressed their inked thumbs to the paper. The fourth grew hysterical and bolted, but even as he fled he managed to carry away a full leg dripping with fat and a length of gut which he wore around his neck as a ritual garland. Kotharami and old Pallivela-achchan gave chase. Over the fields and across the stream they ran, a few villagers joining the hunt. But the moment the Chakkiliya reached the outcast settlement he turned on them defiant, the chopper knife in his right hand, the leg of meat in his left and the gut around his neck, like the Mother Goddess after slaying the Buffalo Demon. The dogs of the settlement lined up behind him. They did not bark, they merely bared their teeth in evil intent. Behind this martial row of dogs lined up a hundred Chakkiliya women and behind them the dim shapes of the outcast vampires.

Kotharami, Pallivela-achchan and the villagers turned back in defeat. By the time Pallivela-achchan got back to Kalyani-achchi's house, where the head of the buffalo, its horns held high, lay atop a heap of hide, he was faint with exhaustion. The soles of his feet were studded with thorns from the chase. Pangi tended his wounds with the white man's medicine.

'Be not anxious, O Pallivela-achchan,' he said.

But the old man, exhausted, his feet smarting, was distraught. 'We haven't got the thumbprint of the fourth outcast,' he moaned. 'Will the company pay me less for it?'

Pangi was seized of the problem. The white man's law was unrelenting, on earth as it was in heaven. The absence of the thumb impression was bound to reduce the policy money by a fourth. But perhaps there was a way out. The whole of Playini could thumbprint a mass petition to the Inspector. Or better still, they could use the law to attach the homestead of the recalcitrant outcast. This last suggestion scared Pallivela-achchan. If they brought the law on the Chakkiliya, the rest of the Chakkiliyas would gang up behind him; they had their dogs and vampires. Nothing would happen to Pangi, as he had the protection of the white man, but he, Pallivela-achchan, would be defenceless. Pangi, finally set him at rest, by promising to compensate him from his personal funds.

The next morning Pangi sought out Pallivela-achchan and enquired if there were taxpayers in the village. There were two. Mannadiar, the landlord, and Mayilvahana Pandaram, the man of the mendicant caste who made money honing glass splinters into costume jewellery. But they lived outside the village territory. Pangi said that it did not matter; the company's regulations merely laid down that the remains of the animal should be kept in front of a taxpayer's house because in the company's view those who remitted money to the Crown were the only ones who had legitimacy in the white man's courts of law. Buffalo meat was unclean to the upper caste Hindu and Mannadiar sent word that any attempt to bring the unclean remains to his farm would be resisted with knives. Pallivela-achchan almost dropped dead. 'You don't have to give up,' Pangi said. 'There is one more taxpayer after all.' The mendicant community was an immigrant minority, timid and reluctant to fight. Pangi reasoned that Mayilvahana Pandaram would not resist. Thus a large crowd, carrying the buffalo's head, moved towards Mayilvahana Pandaram's house. Leading them, supporting himself on a staff, walked Chippu-achchan the village elder.

The maker of jewels protested weakly, 'O Chippu, why do you bring this damnation on me?'

'You call this damnation?' the elder retorted. 'This is a mandate of the white man's law.'

Thus was installed at the jeweller's gate the horned symbol of death. After sundown the onlookers and helpers dispersed, and Pallivela-achchan lit his lantern and began an all-night wake. He took a bottle of spirit from his satchel and drank. He had been drinking since afternoon, to soften the pain in the soles of his feet. But within him was a deeper pain that grew with the drink. The buffalo's eyes were wide open, and he felt them on him. He remembered when it was a motherless calf, he had fed it milk and covered it with blankets during the cold. Whenever he passed the cattle shed it would lift its horned head and give a grunt of recognition. After it had grazed, it would come home on its own and if Pallivela-achchan was seated on the outer plinth, would lay its head on his lap to be scratched and petted. When Pallivela-achchan lost his little patch of land, with no ploughing to be done, he no longer needed the animal. The young buffalo had an inauspicious whorl, and so Pallivela-achchan could find no buyers. He could only sell it to the butcher and the butcher paid very little. It was then that the disease struck. In pain the animal sought out its master, and pleaded with its large eyes of opal, *save me, father! I do not want to leave you.* Love and the lure of quick money contended inside Pallivela-achchan; greed prevailed. Stealthily, he had emptied the bowl of medicament into the hedge; his wife had brewed it and it might have saved the animal... Pallivela-achchan drank again from the bottle, and groggy with drink and penitence, caressed the swollen and greasy head, the horns and wide open eyes. Tears streamed down his eyes. *Son,* he said, *forgive me. My days are numbered, and I too am coming.*

The next day each gust of wind that blew through Playini was laden with the scent of death which thundered on the roofs of thatch like a stampede of invisible buffaloes. It was eight days since the vigil had begun and Mayilvahana Pandaram was crazed by the presence at the gate. Swarms of flies landed on his house, and sombre shadows glided across his yard as the vigilant vultures circled above. In frenzied despair the jewel-maker screamed and ranted and undid his tuft. Pallivela-achchan's anger now turned on Mayilvahana Pandaram.

'I'm keeping vigil here,' he said, 'I'm holding out for justice. Why do you make it unpleasant for me?'

'O Pallivelan,' Mayilvahana Pandaram said, 'how will you get your money if you squat here?'

'You are the taxpayer...'

'I'm not the only one. Couldn't you have dumped this at Mannadiar's gate?'

'You want to get me stabbed by Mannadiar's toughs?'

'Do you want us to suffocate?'

Pallivela-achchan could take it no more. 'O immigrant,' he said, 'you keep out of this. This is blood money. One more word, and you'll drive me mad.'

It was midnight. There was no moon, the dark winds filled the palmyra leaves. Through this blind night, the pedal machine moved along the mud track to Palghat town... It was the ninth morning, there was yet no sign of the Inspector. Pangi was not to be seen either. The villagers thought that he had gone in search of the Inspector.

*

But another happening blotted the buffalo's death from the minds of people; the body of a woman dangling from a mango tree before the temple. The villagers gathered, they looked on and were startled. It was Kalyani-achchi. The women of Playini went to console the orphaned daughter. They found Pangi's corridor empty. Pangi had removed his belongings in the night and left Playini forever. It was many months later that the villagers managed to get a lawyer to examine the printed documents with which they had insured their cattle. They discovered that the papers had nothing to do with the fabulous enterprise beyond the seas, but were old tabulation sheets of the evangelist school at Palghat. These, besides the accumulated dues in Narayana Tharakan's tea-shop, and a large wooden cross, were all that reminded Playini of the short-lived return of its prodigal son.

A week after Kalyani-achchi's death policemen descended on Playini. Children fled and sought shelter. Without warning the policemen went berserk, breaking pots of clay and bronze. They went waist-deep into the tank and gazing at the women bathing bare-breasted, indulged in the horrific act of self-abuse. Then they made their way, drenched and wretched, to Kalyani-achchi's grave and dug out the body. Many villagers saw it. The body had not decayed, it had strangely become more beautiful. They had buried her without ornaments, clothed in a length of unbleached cotton. But when they exhumed her, she was naked, with an enormous copper crucifix around her neck.

The policemen and the villagers stood a long while around the naked corpse, yet it occurred to no one to drape her.

They had never seen such a spectacle before; large black nipples like *rudraksha* beads, thighs of *sandal*, a motherly waist, and down which spread beneath her navel like a black sunrise. The men stood gazing on. They could not free themselves from this vision and were punished for their act of lust with an impotence that lasted the rest of their lives.

Towards dusk, fastened to bamboo and accompanied by plumes and torches, Kalyani-achchi embarked on her journey to the town. Many villagers, including the Chakkiliyas, were forced to go with the corpse. All had to print their thumbs on the yellow parchments of the State. In the hospital the doctors cut open Kalyani-achchi's stomach. There, like a crouching possum, lay a half-grown foetus.

The Sacred Eagle

In summer the river dried into white beds of sand, with slender filaments of blue flowing down these to the sea. Farmers would claim their lots on the sand to raise the gold-coloured cucumber. We children would walk upstream, trudging along on the cool moist sand, feeling the summer cool on the river. If we walked on past the banyans which stretched their branches over the sands, past the embankments of ancient moss and fern, we would come to the blue foothills. But we did not dare go beyond these to where the river sprang from a rock crevice in the mountain. Instead we were content with the magic terrors of the nearness of the wild. Walking all day we the truants would time our return home by the school's evening bell. It was on this return journey that we would crowd into the coffee–shop of Shivarama Pattar, the Brahmin. Not for coffee, which we could not afford, but for a draught of water which we really did not need.

'So you did not go to school today, did you?' Shivarama Pattar would chide us mischievously, gleeful at having caught us in our truancy.

We were afraid that Shivarama Pattar might tell our parents, yet were reassured that he probably would not.

'What did you see?' Shivarama Pattar would often enquire.

'We saw the great banyan.'

'Did you see the nest of the sacred eagle?'

'No.'

'Well, you need grace for that.'

The Brahmin settlement was a string of contiguous houses that lay parallel to the river. Shivarama Pattar's coffee-shop was at one extremity of the settlement. Our village was made up of this settlement and a few scattered feudal manors, and its skies were choked with the green of arching jack and mango branches. Today the village is rich, the green arches of jack and mango have given way to funnels that spew smoke, and the pacific noises of old to the rasping converse of trade. But to me the single major punctuation of change was the setting up of the pathologist's laboratory which peered down through microscopes into our blood and phlegm and excrement. With its coming was lost the privacy of the village, though it also gave us a weird security. There was no room for sentiment in this strength, but old Shivarama Pattar still haunts me, I think of his desolate cry as he walked along the river bed and disappeared.

Today that little house, which was both Shivarama Pattar's home and coffee-shop, is falling into gentle dilapidation. In its dank spaces march moth and cockroach, the rearguard of a great withdrawal. Concrete houses with steel and glass windows bear down on the shop. Shivarama Pattar's well, from which we drew water in our childhood to quench our schoolboys' feigned thirst, is still full, though Dakshayani-amma, the pathologist, wanted it filled with earth. A hidden tributary of the river perennially fed the well with crystal water. Today the river is drier than before but the hidden tributary still replenishes the well. Yet no one drinks from it, as the village has piped water coming from the dam far away.

Shivarama Pattar remains a staple memory of my childhood. The glass facade of the shop and the sacred oil lamp, the leftover sweets which he occasionally kept for us, his loving taunts about our truancy; these were the vignettes of our growing up.

Before leaving for the city of Madras to pursue my studies, I visited Shivarama Pattar. 'Kuttan,' he said, 'study well and come back a big man.' He untied and tied again his Brahmin's tuft and watched me with gentle eyes. It was like the days of my childhood again, the days of the walks upstream. Shivarama Pattar had many things to say about the city of Madras, about his kinsmen who had migrated from the village to that city and settled in its colonies of Triplicane and Mandavalli and become aliens. Shivarama Pattar gave me the names of some of them and said they would certainly welcome me, they would remember the river which sprang from the great cliff of rock where the sacred eagle nested. As we sat talking his two young children played marbles in the yard.

'I wish they would study well,' Shivarama Pattar said, 'but they are so indolent.'

'After all they are children, aren't they?' I consoled him.

'Do you remember, Kuttan, the days when I used to keep crisp *murukkus* for you and the other children? That was all I hoped to do with this coffee-shop. But times are changing, and profit has made its presence felt in the village. I hope these children too are not consumed by the lure of profit. I hope they do not become immigrants and aliens.'

Just then the brown and white eagle sacred to Krishna whistled and circled overhead.

'Krishna, Krishna!' Shivarama Pattar said. 'Kuttan, Lord Krishna has blessed you. Go and prosper.'

Shivarama Pattar handed me a parcel. I knew what it contained: *murukkus* which aunt Vishalam had made for me to take to Madras. Holding it in my hands, I heard the fried ringlets crackle, I heard the pattering footfall of truant children. Aunt Vishalam peeped out of the door and smiled, 'Kuttan, will you take some pickle as well?'

'No, aunt, it is slightly messy to carry.'

'Vishalam does not know a thing about the city,' Shivarama Pattar spoke indulgently, as he would of a daughter. Aunt Vishalam was thirty-five and Shivarama Pattar sixty. Yet the elaborate observances of the Brahmin had kept his body healthful and clean. He hoped to carry on in this state of well-being for another twenty years, chanting the *gayatri* and repeating the thousand attributes of the Lord and attending to his *karma* of making *vadas* and *iddlies*.

*

Every summer I visited the village. I did not forget to report to Shivarama Pattar on his kinsmen in Triplicane and Mandavalli.

'They have left home and become aliens,' Shivarama Pattar said. 'But we stayed here and have become aliens in our own village.'

In a vast circle around the village rose the structures of steel, glass and cement, prosperous, abundant, and accepted by all the village. My old class-fellow Janardhanan with whom I had once walked the river was proud of this growth, proud of being part of it. He said to me by way of a taunt, 'You go back to Madras after the summer, don't you?'

'Yes.'

'You are not done with your education yet? How much more time to go?'

I told him how long I would need to complete my Bachelor's and go on to my Master's.

'What do you get out of all this?' Janardhanan said. 'Look at me. In just six months I have learnt to examine blood and phlegm and excrement. It was Dakshayani-amma who taught me. Kuttan, do you want your phlegm examined?'

The absurdity of the offer did not register on me, so abruptly was it thrown up. Janardhanan chattered enthusiastically about the laboratory. Dakshayani-amma owned it. She was its principal chemist as well. Dakshayani-amma was of the same age as aunt Vishalam. Aunt Vishalam was fair, while Dakshayani-amma was dark and sultry, an irresistibly attractive black. Janardhanan was an employee of the laboratory, but it was not merely wages that tied him to the institution, it was the spell of that pungent body. Janardhanan described it, aroused by each detail, the black lips flashing smiles of pearl, the mascara spreading on to the cheeks, the stain of sweat as she walked up and down the laboratory.

'I have seen her blood in the microscope,' Janardhanan said. 'She showed it to me. She has promised to show everything.'

I listened to the story of the microscope as I would to an account of the disrobing of that intimidating woman. We walked down the settlement, the leaves of the trees that remained quivered in the river wind. Janardhanan was immersed, aroused, frenetic, in the story of his microscopes.

'Kuttan, isn't it Thursday tomorrow?'

'Yes, the day sacred to Krishna.'

The sacred eagle was in the sky again. Janardhanan looked up in anger, then picking up a twig from the ground, hurled it futilely at the bird.

'The day sacred to Krishna, pooh!' Janardhanan said. 'It is tomorrow, Thursday, that Dakshayani-amma has promised to show me her phlegm.'

*

The years went by. After my Master's and my doctoral dissertation, I became a wanderer, seeking jobs and positions. I was in a far country, and so was not by the bedside of my mother and later my father when they died...

I returned to the village after my long exile. As I stepped into our ancient home, the scents of its woodwork roused my childhood memories, my alienation was gone.

'Your room has been kept in readiness for your coming,' Govindan Nair, the old caretaker, informed me. There was nothing ready about the house, it was beset by dust and termites. I walked through the house and stepped into the backyard. The scene was unfamiliar.

'Govindan Nair,' I asked, 'where are the mango and jack trees?'

'They were cut down. For the cremation.'

I gazed on at the stretch of land at the back, not merely had the mango and jack vanished but there was no trace of the numberless orchard trees or even the flower beds. They had all been cleared away. I pressed the question. Reluctantly Govindan Nair answered, 'Well, I myself decided to clear them, because...' He held back his words, hesitant.

'Tell me, Govindan Nair.'

'Oh,' Govindan Nair said, still hesitant, 'she said she would rent this house if we cleared the trees and the bushes. In any case you don't intend living here, do you?'

'Rent this house? Who?'

In an awed whisper, as though uttering a charmed word, he said, 'Dakshayani-amma.'

I did not know what to make of the proposition. The house, a sprawling feudal mansion, was difficult to maintain. Govindan Nair was a decrepit old man, a malingerer full of corroding vices, slipping faster into desuetude than the house itself.

'Kuttan,' Govindan Nair said.

'Yes, Govindan Nair?'

The awed whisper again, 'Dakshayani-amma examined my phlegm.'

A strange look came over Govindan Nair's face, more squalid than putrid phlegm.

'Kuttan...'

'What is it now, Govindan Nair?'

'Do you want your phlegm examined?'

I put an end to the bizarre conversation. Govindan Nair withdrew to his quarters, sullen. I retired to my chamber upstairs and tried to rest, but was deeply disturbed by the old caretaker's transformation. Over the backyard, cruelly stripped of all vegetation, hung a pall of heat. Neither bird nor dragonfly sought noontide refuge there as of old. And in the burning skies above there was no more the sacred eagle, wheeling round in gentle circles.

After a while, unrested, I got out and walked to the Brahmin settlement. As I walked down in the barren heat I recalled the water of Shivarama Pattar's well with its herbal aromas. Presently I was at Shivarama Pattar's door. 'Aunt Vishalam!' I called.

She peered out, and when she saw me, was exuberant. 'It is you, my Kuttan! When did you come?'

'Today, a little while ago. Where is Shivarama Pattar?'

She was dispirited as she answered me, 'He went away yesterday, to the temple at Thiruvalathur. He sits there in prayer, and will return the day after.'

It was then I noticed the glass-fronted shelves were empty, neither the *iddlies* that Shivarama Pattar made nor aunt Vishalam's *murukkus* filling them.

'Aunt Vishalam,' I asked, apprehensive, 'why are the shelves empty?'

She mopped her eyes with the end of her saree. She said, 'We have closed shop. They discovered a germ in our well water. What can you say against the evidence of the microscope?'

'They discovered a germ? Who?'

'Dakshayani-amma.'

Adversity was overtaking aunt Vishalam. My thoughts went to her sons Ambi and Chuppamani. I enquired after them.

'Oh, you have been away,' she said. 'Much has happened in these years. Ambi is in Vishakhapatnam, working as a factory hand.'

'Well, that is good for him.'

Aunt Vishalam looked at me, gently accusing. 'He is fated to be a factory-hand,' she said. 'And fated, too, to marry a girl from that far place, a bride who does not speak our language or worship our gods. Yet I wrote to him that I would accept her, but Ambi does not want to show his face in the village. He has become an alien. And Chuppamani...' Aunt Vishalam began to cry. 'My poor Chuppamani, he walked out one day two years ago and has not been heard of since. His father goes into retreat in the temple and prays for him.'

Words of consolation failed me, and I sat in her presence in silence. When I stepped out into the street again I felt the oppressive heat of steel and cement over the ancient settlement. The houses of the Brahmins lay desolate, the stucco crumbling off their fronts; vestments of once precious silk put out to dry lay derelict. Behind the settlement rose the giant structures of steel and glass with their clangour of prosperity, the machine-shops, the weaving centres, the video parlours. And dominating it all was the laboratory, a malefic sentinel over the secret fluids of the village. In this tumult of growth Shivarama Pattar's coffee-shop had closed, and Ambi and Chuppamani had left the village never to come back.

I was sick when I got home. In the evening I called on the *vaidyan*, our traditional healer. He felt my pulse, and recited a verse from an ancient text of medicine. 'It is your mind that is afflicted, Kuttan. Your body needs no medicine.'

It was true that I was suffering for my village, for its denuded earth, and for its old monastic habitats oppressed by burgeoning steel and cement. I returned from the *vaidyan* and lay down on my bed. Govindan Nair came into my chamber.

'You do not look all right,' he said officiously.

'It will pass, Govindan Nair, with a little rest.'

Once again the strange contortion came over Govindan Nair's face. 'I cannot let you lie like this,' he said. 'I must get your phlegm examined.'

'I can take care of myself,' I said. 'Now you go back to your room.'

The sternness in my voice restored him to the habit of compliance and he withdrew. I rested. For the next two days I did not leave the house, and spent most of the time in bed. On the second day at noon Janardhanan, my class-fellow, paid me a visit. He came like a blast of noontide heat, and would have none of the pleasantries which friends meeting after so long would naturally exchange. He had come to bully me into supporting a plan of his.

'You do not know what is going on here,' he said. 'It is subversion. But we have decided not to let it go on anymore.'

'Let what go on? 'I asked in incomprehension.

'It is Dakshayani-amma's decision. She has seen it all in the microscope.'

'Seen what, Janardhanan?'

'The microbes.'

'Where?'

'In that Brahmin's coffee-shop, in his well, in his kitchen, on his walls and pillars. There are microbes all over. They are there in his woman's rotten silks. Dakshayani-amma has shown them to me, microbes that have red eyes and fly like bats.'

'Get a hold on yourself, Janardhanan.'

'This is not the time for peace. The house of this Brahmin must be demolished. But Dakshayani-amma is deterred by the old man's spells, he goes to Thiruvalathur and prays.'

'Let the old Brahmin pray, Janardhanan. How does it hurt you?'

'He is praying against science. It is sabotage. It is occult. But mark my words, the microscope will triumph.'

I got up from my bed to offer him a lemonade, which he refused. 'Don't you think you are imagining things, Janardhanan?' I reasoned with him. 'A flying microbe shaped like a bat is unheard of.'

The contortion, the pathologist's frenzy, came over Janardhanan's face, as it had on Govindan Nair's a while ago. 'Who can dispute what I have seen?' he said. 'I saw them flap their wings. I heard them too. Dakshayani-amma told me, *meditate, Janardhanan, meditate like that Brahmin and listen*. Then I heard them cry *kwa, kwa*, like the water-fowl.'

'In the microscope?'

'Of course, where else?'

I was in no mood to laugh. I was distressed. I said, 'Nobody will believe this, Janardhanan, a microbe which cries out like the water-fowl.'

'They all believe it. In the weaving shed, in the machine-shop, everywhere.'

'Trust me, can't you? I have studied the microbe at college, and nowhere have I come across a screaming microbe with bat's wings.'

Janardhanan rose, shivering. 'Upstart!' he said. 'You and your damned education!' He lunged at me, fingers outspread in feline violence. I moved aside, and reprimanded him severely.

He quietened. 'I am sorry,' he said.

'It doesn't matter.'

Janardhanan left the house like a stranger.

Over the village the heat lay, white hot, convex. Presently it was afternoon, yet the heat did not abate. There were a few claps of thunder in the rainless sky… I sent Govindan Nair to find out if Shivarama Pattar had returned from the temple. He had not.

In the evening when Govindan Nair brought me my coffee, I told him, 'I shall not eat tonight.'

'Are you ill, Kuttan?'

'I am all right, I want to rest. Don't disturb me at night.'

'As you wish.'

I slept beneath that relentless canopy of heat. The heat continued into the night, the stars were hot. I was woken at midnight by a cry, soon I was wide awake and listening. The cry came from the river sands. I got out of my bed, climbed down the stairs and rushed to the riverside. The cry came again, aunt Vishalam's cry!

Over the dark sand, in the filigree of the river, the reflected stars were a spangle of silver. The water was like the stilled lace of lightning stretching seaward. The riverbed was full of people. They had come from the weaving shed and the machine shop and the video den, called out by Janardhanan. It was they who had chased aunt Vishalam to the river.

'*Ayyo*, Janardhanan!' I cried.

I fancied Janardhanan turned to look at me for a brief instant.

'Desist, Janardhanan,' I said.

'Who are you to interfere? Her blouse and saree are full of bats!'

Aunt Vishalam tripped as she ran, now she was prostrate on the sand. I saw Janardhanan's hands grip her hair, then tug at her clothes.

'Don't, my son, don't !' aunt Vishalam cried.

'Lie still, you bitch!' Janardhanan screamed. 'Let us get the bats out!'

The mob ringed them round, hysterical. Janardhanan unwound her saree, roll after roll; the mob cheered. There was an enormous streak of lightning, and in its light I saw aunt Vishalam, disrobed, beautiful, unresisting as a corpse. I turned away from the sin of that seeing. I floundered back over rock and thicket.

I crawled into my bed, and in my foetal refuge a swoon came over me. My dreams were like waking vision. We walked on the river again. We walked past the blue foothills into the teeming forest and came to the rock crevice near the summit from which the river sprang in joyful tumult. Above the spring in a magic castle of twigs nestled Krishna's eagle, the white ring about his throat shimmering in the forest gloom. When I woke again it was noon. Govindan Nair stood anxiously by my bedside.

'Are you better, Kuttan?' he asked.

'Mm.'

'Did you know, Kuttan, there was a cloudburst in the mountains. But the river is still dry.'

'Mm.'

'Shall I get your coffee?'

'No. Just leave me alone.'

Then a dreamless sleep. Again at midnight the cry, another cry. Like a somnambulist I rose and went to the river. Shivarama Pattar was wandering over the sands in search of his Vishalam. And, suddenly, ripping the earth a deep, angry roar. Govindan Nair had followed me. In obscene delight he exclaimed, 'Kuttan, Kuttan! It is the cloudburst!' The dark flood of the mountain thundered down the river, it swallowed Shivarama Pattar, then moved on and the riverbed was quiet again. Terror overcame me and I curled up on the river bank.

The skies of the river grew red with day-break. High above rose an unearthly whistle of pain. It shrilled down the length of the river. I looked up. It was the eagle. And bats were in the sky, monstrous bats with red eyes which saw clearly by the fiery light of day.

The bats hunted the sacred eagle.

Renuka

Renuka of the legends, her name meaning dust-begotten or pollen woman, was the wife of the sage Jamadagni. She was so chaste that she could fetch water from the river without a pitcher; the water would form itself into a crystal ball which she would carry home. One day, witnessing the thousand-armed king Karthaveeryarjuna at play with his consorts in the river, Renuka experienced a moment of frailty. The water refused to form into a crystal ball that day and she carried it home in a pitcher. The sage knew this, and asked who of his seven sons would punish the mother with death. Only the youngest, Parasurama, came forward. He beheaded his mother with a battleaxe. Pleased, the sage asked him what boon he wanted. Parasurama asked for his mother. Jamadagni brought Renuka back to life.

'The wind is coming,' the girl clad in bark called into the cave. Inside the cave, her father, Purandara, broke his meditation, and lifted his gaze up towards the portal. 'Come inside, Surabhi,' he said.

The wind was still far away. Its yellow was lit by the sunset, and shone golden across the wilderness. Surabhi stood on the ridge of rock that ringed the cave's mouth, gazing upon the approaching tide of colour with fascination. Above her skirt of bark her breasts were the colour of *sandal*, a rich fawn. Guiltily, she thought the colour of the wind more beautiful. From inside the cave Purandara called out again, 'Come inside, my daughter.'

'I'm coming.'

Purandara waited, Surabhi was still on the ridge.

He called out again, 'Surabhi, don't watch the wind. Your will might falter.'

'It will not, my father.'

Yet she stayed on the ridge. The wind billowed forward, even from a distance its forbidden pollens casting their glow on the ridge. The voice of her father was tinged with gentle alarm, 'Beware of the wind, my daughter. It is temptation.'

The wind, through myriad crystal explosions of chemical amalgams, flung jewels into the sky. The jewels glittered in the sunset.

'I'm tending the *thumbas*,' Surabhi lied.

The lie grew within her, like a foetus conceived in stealth, she gloried in its sensual secrecy. Yet she grieved over her disobedience.

*

In the cave, Purandara uneasily recalled an evening sixteen springs ago. Surabhi was a nurseling. Laying her down on the soft grass of the cave, Sharmishta, his wife, had gone up on to the ridge to watch the wind. Waking out of his meditation he called out to her, 'Sharmishta, what are you doing?'

'The wind is coming.'

'Let it.'

'Let me stay here awhile, and watch the wind.'

Purandara fell silent. After a while he called out again, 'Is your will faltering?'

In the silence that ensued, Purandara sensed her fear and fascination; Sharmishta said, 'No. I'm merely watching its splendrous colours. It is far away, and I shall get back to the cave before it reaches us.'

'Watch it if it pleases you. But remember it is merely a cloud of chemical dust which the City of the Mutants blows over our peaceful caves.'

'The yellow wind gleams like gold in the sun. On its upper reaches the chemicals glitter like jewels.'

'Sharmishta, you speak in feebleness! Why does the yellow wind charm you so? Think of the rich fawn of our bodies, and of the child our great desires have given birth to.'

There was no answer from the ridge, and so Purandara asked after a while, 'What else do you see?'

Sharmishta answered hesitantly, 'The wind approaches, and in its yellow expanse I see…' Again, silence.

The meditating mind had seen it all; yet Purandara said, 'Describe it to me, and speak without fear.'

'I see three mutants, a female and two males.'

Purandara was sad. *The sin of Renuka is on my woman*, he said to himself.

'Sharmishta, what else do you see?'

'A monstrous love play. The male mutants are tying up the

female with great tentacles. I hear her laugh.'

'Come down and shut the portals of the cave.'

She did not do so. On the floor of the cave, the little child, Surabhi, grew restless and cried; Purandara stroked her hands and feet, and she grew quiet.

'Sharmishta, what are you doing?'

'I shall be down in a little while.'

Still she stood on the ridge. As the wind blew over their grasslands, the cave filled with its whistling.

'Sharmishta, make haste!'

She did not reply. The wind roared and over its noises Purandara heard laughter. The laughter of the mutants, and the laughter of the sage's wife as she watched the love play of the demon king. A burst of wind slammed shut the slab of rock that covered the cave's mouth.

'Ah, Sharmishta!'

Over the closed portals of the cave, across the grasslands, the wind played in eddies. Purandara still heard Sharmishta's laughter. Presently he heard her tremulous crying, 'Ah, I can endure this no more!'

The chemicals hung over the grasslands in dense clouds, blotting out the sky. As Sharmishta struggled for breath, the male mutants wound their tentacles round her, she writhed in their stench and slime.

'Oxygen-breather, primitive,' one of the mutant said, 'we shall teach you to breathe the blissful chemical vapours. Look at our beautiful teeth, they are not, like yours, inside our mouths. They circle our faces like pearl garlands. And from them ooze sensuous spit and phlegm...'

'Mercy!'

'Look, primitive ! A third of our bodies is chemical, yet another third is machine and only the rest is flesh. Once upon a time we too breathed oxygen like you, and were content with diminutive genitals and brief orgasms, we bore our young in sacks of flesh and not in crystal globes. But science freed us from nature. Obstinate cave-dweller, why do you hold out against progress? Look at our metallic phalluses...'

'Mercy!'

'Here, if you swallow this capsule, just this one, you too will be transformed like us, transformed in an instant. Distilled in this capsule is centuries of learning, the magic of transformation, the revolution.'

Renuka's chastity cried out in Sharmishta, 'I do not need it. I am content with my body and my husband and my child.'

'You slander science!'

'Free me!'

'You have insulted the chemicals. In the name of human progress, we punish you!'

The mutant raised its tentacles and invoked the anger of the cloud, and from the murky skies the thunder descended on her. Inside the cave Purandara heard its clatter, then heard it die away in rumbling echoes. Around the portal of the cave the remains of Sharmishta lay scattered, a few fistfuls of chemical pollen.

*

The memories of times past came back to Purandara, insistent, alarming. He called out to his daughter again, 'Surabhi, come back inside.'

Her lie about the *thumba* beds now grew into a sorrowing truth inside Surabhi, and she looked on the flowers in frenetic caring.

'Father,' she cried, 'the *thumbas* are withering in the blast.'

'They will sprout again, my daughter. The plant survives the chemical and the machine better than we ever can. Come down.'

Once again, her frailty returning, Surabhi was charmed by the splendour of chemical pigment; she despaired over the living fawn of her skin, the colour of fragrant *sandal*.

It was during the last full moon that Krishna and she had walked on the grass. No cloud obscured the moon, and in the grass it lit below the insects chirped softly.

Surabhi held the hand of her betrothed. 'The moon is full inside me.'

Their arms twined and Krishna sensed her pungent nearness.

'Krishna,' she said, 'let me shed my skirt of bark.'

' Have patience, beloved.'

' Don't you want to see my thighs and navel shine in the moon?'

Krishna wound a tender hand around her waist. ' This body

is for me, kept in troth. And so is mine for you.'

Surabhi's lips parted, hungering wet.

'Wait,' Krishna said, 'for our vows to come to fruition, for the moment when you and I will become one flesh in the presence of the sacrificial fire.'

Surabhi answered with a wild embrace, and, overcoming his resistance, began planting deep kisses on his lips. 'O Krishna, are not my lips sweet?' She undid her tresses and tossed them around him. Then she flung aside her skirt and stood naked in the moon.'Krishna, touch me.'

'I wait in prayer for the touch,' he said. 'I shall wait until your father, my teacher, lights the sacred fire.'

'Are you dissatisfied, Krishna? Do you prefer the gold of the chemical to the *sandal* of my skin?'

'God is my witness...'

She stood dispirited over the skirt of bark. Far away, in the silt of the horizon, the citadel of science smouldered, its line of lights the ornament around a monster of the dark.

'Krishna,' Surabhi said, 'I've kept it a secret, but the chemicals unsettle my peace.'

Krishna trembled, and Surabhi broke down and wept, 'Save me, Krishna. Forbidden desires come to me, they fill me unbearably. Are you content with my humanness? I am not, I want to have my flower of desire as large as those of the female mutants. I want to experience the orgasm of the machine.'

'God!'

*

Surabhi lingered on in sensuous transgression, she lingered on at the mouth of the cave. Purandara sank back into meditation and sorrowed, *God, it is the curse of Renuka coming back.* The first whiff of the invading fumes touched the *thumbas*. Surabhi sorrowed for the flowers, yet she looked on the billowing cloud with forbidden expectancy. Beneath the cloud's canopy of diamond and topaz dust, she saw the prancing mutants, two males and a female.

In the cave Purandara froze in the intense awareness of meditation.

The clouds swept over Surabhi with the howl of a thousand

trumpets. The lust of the male mutants spilled, tempestuous, over the female. From the teeth around their faces oozed copious spit and phlegm.

' Primitive,' one of the male mutants spoke to Surabhi, 'are you not tired of breathing oxygen?'

' I am tired,' Surabhi said.

' Do you not covet the orgasm of the machine?'

Surabhi was wet with the fluids of sin. She said, 'I do, I do!'

'You cherish the chemical. You understand liberation.'

'I understand.'

The images came to her mind, disintegrating even as they came, of her meditating father and celibate lover. The mutant prised her lips open and slipped in the magic capsule. The physic of liberation melted on her tongue, it seeped into her farthest capillaries, splintering into a myriad precious stones. Laughter shook her, hysterical, and as she laughed, her teeth pushed themselves out, limning her face with a garland of pearl. Three eyes opened on her forehead, her chest was now burdened with four prodigious breasts, the *sandal* of her skin gave way to flaming gold. Her brain turned to chemical polymer, bones to metal. Her flower of lust split open, cavernous, and the male mutants entered.

Waking out of the stupor, Surabhi felt her new eyes and breasts and flower. She asked , 'Who am I?'

The male mutant replied, 'You were a primitive monster. Science has liberated you and made you human.'

In the sky overhead hung the glittering mutant twilight.

The chemical vapours filled her lungs. Inside the cave Purandara's meditation became *yogic* fire. It seared Surabhi.

'Help me!' she cried. 'I want to be human again.'

'But you are human, you have become one. You were animal before.'

The penitence of Renuka filled her, the cry for reprieve.

'Let me be an animal again. Let me have my two breasts and colour of *sandal* back. Restore me to Krishna!'

The mutants held her in their tentacles. The mutants laughed. The capsule overcame the last resistant cell.

'Beautiful one,' said the mutant, 'you will get over this frailty, soon you will celebrate the liberation.'

She broke loose from the slimy tentacles and fled. All round her, and into the uttermost distance, the wind howled yellow.

She floundered through it in search of her lost animalhood, lamenting loud, an unredeemed Renuka.

*

Purandara and Krishna came out of the cave to survey the devastation. The cloud, its fury spent, now billowed down and seeped like a toxic breath through the grasses. Within Purandara burned the life-giving flame, the sage's will, and to this Krishna turned in prayer. Pleased, Purandara, like Jamadagni, asked.

'Son, what boon do you seek?'

Krishna's gaze moved away from the sage to the annihilated earth: the once verdant, flowering, fruitful earth, mother earth. In tears, in ecstasy, Krishna sought the boon, 'My mother!'

THE STREAM OF HARMONY

The Little Ones

The compound bounding our farmhouse was extensive. It sloped down to the south towards the paddy fields, and where it met cultivated land was a hedge full of fruit trees—citrus, pomegranate and guava. Near the hedge was the little hut where old Nagandi-appan, our farm manager, lived. We spoke of him as the manager merely from the persistence of memory, for he had long since ceased to manage the farm. Nagandi-appan's wife and son were dead, and the old man lived on in the farm as a part of its environment. We, the children, who had always seen him on the farm believed that he would be there for all time.

Every evening Nagandi-appan walked along the paddy ridges, as he had in the days when he tended the crops. But he no longer looked after stile or waterway, he carried neither spade nor lantern, he merely walked the ridges. During these journeys, he carried with him a small earthen pot full of palm brew left over from his sundown drinking. He paused every now and then to sprinkle this over the ridges. Neither my father nor mother took notice of this ritual of many years. As a matter of fact, no one in the farm took notice of anything, nor did anyone do anything to manage it, and this included my father; in this state of happy indifference the paddy and the orchard and the cattle grew in fullness and health.

Nagandi-appan was fond of us children. He procured for us forbidden sweets, crude sugar shaped into pencils and onions, peasant delicacies. We went to his hut when the lamps were lit, and sat before him to hear his stories. These, he reminded us, were true: poltergeists encountered in the fields, winged tortoises which dived in and out of streams and tiny serpents who mocked his faltering steps. My sister Ramani and I found these stories more real than our lessons in history.

'Nagandi-appan,' Ramani asked him once, 'what colour are these serpents?'

'Aw,' Nagandi-appan said, 'some are gold, some are silver, and others, turquoise.'

We sat lost in a festival of little snakes, magical and capricious. 'Nagandi-appan,' Ramani asked, 'will these serpents come out to play?'

'Of course, they will.'

'Then shall we call them?'

Nagandi-appan smiled sadly. He said, 'The time is not yet.'

There was no place in Nagandi-appan's story for why it was not yet time. There were no questions in our contented lives, nor in the story of how our farm prospered unmanaged and untended. We spent the greater part of the evening listening to Nagandi-appan and went back home reluctantly for supper. After this we were too tired to open our books. Thus was our education unmanaged and untended like the farm, with neither recitation nor revision.

'My children,' Nagandi-appan once said, 'you will become big and important people. I have done something to ensure that.'

'What, Nagandi-appan?'

'You don't have to pore over your books. They will come and teach you while you sleep.'

'Who?'

Again the quizzical smile, Nagandi-appan said, 'It is not yet time to tell you.'

We grew up. When Ramani came of age she no longer attended the charmed evenings and I went alone to Nagandi-appan's hut. Every night Ramani would have me repeat the stories to her. It was still the poltergeists and tortoises and snakes, but a more mysterious presence now lurked on the fringes of the narration as the days went by. But the time had not yet come for him to tell us what this was. All he did say was that he sprinkled the palm brew to propitiate this presence. Back home we discussed the presence and wondered.

'It must be some creature smaller than a snake, 'Ramani said.

'A kind of pest perhaps,' mother said irreverently.

But it was no laughing matter for us children. 'How can it be a pest?' Ramani demanded.

'It is true,' I said, supporting Ramani. 'Our crops are fine. If Nagandi-appan is feeding the palm brew to pests, how can the paddy grow so well?'

Mother put an end to the dispute. 'Why do you waste your time, my children? Let Nagandi-appan keep whatever little creatures he chooses to.'

*

Now it came about that mother was stricken with a paralytic seizure. One leg grew limp. The *vaidyan* began his ministrations. One evening Nagandi-appan made a sacrificial offering of flower and fruit and palm sugar. I sat watching. After the offering he dipped his finger in the earthen pot and sprinkled the palm brew around the room.

'They will go now,' he said. 'They will go to mother and heal her.'

'Who, Nagandi-appan?' I asked, daring to venture into forbidden country. 'The little ones?'

Reluctantly Nagandi-appan conceded, 'Yes.'

That night I dreamt of Nagandi-appan's little ones, minute creatures, luminous and subtle bodies. I saw swarms of them descend on my mother and enwrap her leg like mist. The *vaidyan* had told us that it would take her three months to get well, but her leg was restored in ten days. Neither mother nor we spoke about the little ones. Nagandi-appan made no more offerings but took his earthen pot out to the fields and there propitiated the little ones with the brew.

There was yet another memorable incident. Ramani was seeking admission to the college of medicine. It was when they called her for the entrance examination that she broke down, she was unprepared.

'I won't make it,' she told me, sobbing. 'They will reject me.'

That evening I went to Nagandi-appan and suggested with a sense of absurdity, 'Nagandi-appan, can you send your little ones somewhere for me?'

'Where to?'

'To the medical college.'

'Of course, I could.'

He made the ritual offering of flower and fruit and palm sugar, then sprinkled the brew in the room. 'My little ones,' he spoke to his invisible host, 'go.'

Sobbing and unprepared, Ramani sat for the test and passed. She enrolled in the college of medicine and in five years was a doctor.

And I started working as a factory engineer. Both of us left the farm and went to faraway towns. Once she confided to me, 'When I make an incision, I don't see anything I learnt in the books of anatomy. Often I marvel how all that gets back into place once again, how it heals.'

'The work of nature, I suppose.'

'I don't know. But it keeps reminding me of Nagandi-appan's little creatures.'

In time our parents died, and there was no one left on the farm except Nagandi-appan who had become brittle with age. The farm looked after itself. On one of my visits home, I found Nagandi-appan bedridden. I sat by his bed and talked about the poltergeists and tortoises and snakes in nostalgia. 'But, Nagandi-appan,' I said, 'one thing remains.'

'What is it, my child?'

'You have not shown me the little ones.'

Nagandi-appan's eyes grew distracted, scanning the far spaces. He clenched his fist, and opening it again read the lines on his palm.

'You have come,' he said, 'at the right time. I shall now show you the little ones.'

'Really, Nagandi-appan?'

'Yes.'

'When, Nagandi-appan?'

He read his palm again, and concentrated.

'Tomorrow night,' he said.

I wondered what the old man had seen in his palm; I felt his forehead. 'Nagandi-appan,' I asked, 'are you very ill?'

Nagandi-appan looked at my face and smiled, contented.

'The breeze,' he said.

'What about the breeze, Nagandi-appan?'

'It blows over me. And it is full of the scent of the wild *tulasi*.' It was a closed room, yet a subtle and aromatic wind, beyond my senses, blew in for Nagandi-appan. Sleep was coming over him, his eyes began to close.

'Rest, Nagandi-appan,' I said.

He looked at me again, intently, and said, 'Let your mind be pure tonight.'

*

In my dreams that night, I sat on a paddy ridge and felt the breeze of the sacred *tulasi*.

The next day, as the dusk darkened over the farm, I went to

the hut. Nagandi-appan had grown even more feeble, he struggled to breathe. 'It is time, my child.'

I gazed on the old face in silent enquiry. Speaking each word with visible effort, he said, 'Go into the compound at the west end and watch the sky.'

I caressed the fevered forehead, and walked out into the compound. I looked to the west. It was a moonless night, and the stars were large and bright. I sent up a childhood prayer, *Little ones, oh my little ones*! Only the stars shone.

Then, slowly, in the far segments of the sky appeared gentle luminescences, soft green and red, glimmering like stardust. They came from the caverns of space rising in infinite multitudes, flying from *mandala* to *mandala* to fulfil the last wish of their high priest. Now they were a deluge, refulgent, dense, another milky way.

God, I said, *Nagandi-appan's little ones*! I raced back to the hut.

'Nagandi-appan,' I cried out as I ran, 'I saw them!'

I entered the hut breathlessly.

'Nagandi-appan, I saw them!'

But the bed was empty.

The Airport

The airport had been long abandoned, the runways had cracked open, exposing the black earth beneath. Lush *konna* bushes grew everywhere, effulgent with golden flowers. No more intimidated by the giant flying machines, moths and beetles returned to these habitats, as did tiny pollen-eating birds and honey-suckers with tubular beaks.

I was a frequent visitor to the airport in its days of traffic. Sometimes to travel, at other times to receive or bid farewell. I was young then, and much given to the pleasure of travel. But as the years passed, the cruising fluids of the body slowed down and cooled, and finally all journeying was replaced by recollection. It was at this time that I came back to the airport, its runways overgrown with *konnas.* I found the place restful and came every evening to sit on the broken steps across the tarmac in the gentle warmth of dilapidation. One evening I became aware that I was not alone, and looking up saw the old man on the step above me. We did not speak at all that evening or the next. But both of us arrived every evening and sat silently each in his place. We were the only people at the airport and I considered our privacies inviolable.

Then one day a honey-sucker was hovering in the *konna* flowers, when a large falcon dropped on it, seized the tiny richly coloured body in its talons and flew off. The old man broke the silence between us for the first time, 'Birds are no better than airplanes.'

'But airplanes offer us no solace the way birds do, 'I said.

The old man grew thoughtful. He said, 'I am no longer sure. Perhaps in times to come airplanes that croon like birds and comfort us will land here.'

I was intrigued, 'But this is no longer an airport. It is a ruin.'

'I have not given up expecting.'

'But where will your airplanes land?'

The old man seemed to pity my ignorance. He said, 'In these bushes. Where else?'

This was our first conversation. We sank back into silence as the ancient twilight darkened, and soon rose and walked our separate ways over the grasses lit by fireflies.

On another evening the old man said, 'So you didn't come yesterday. I was alone.'

'Did you miss me?'

'Not really. As a matter of fact my solitude helped me. I saw him.'

'Saw whom?'

After a long pause, the old man spoke, reluctant, 'Try and experience my solitude.'

Not *my* solitude, but *his* ! I let it pass as an old man's riddle. Again, on yet another evening, he said, 'You don't know what I am waiting for. I shall tell you, if you make an attempt to experience my sorrow.'

'I shall try,' I said.

He said, 'It was from this airport that my son flew away. I come here hoping to catch sight of him again.'

I was baffled, for this was an airport in ruins and neither aircraft nor traveller would use it anymore. I tried to disabuse him of his fantasy as considerately as I could, but he chose not to speak any more of it that evening. For the next few days I did not go to the ruined airport.

When I went again the old man was there. He said, 'Yesterday I saw *him*.'

'You mean he actually returned to this airport?'

After his usual silence the old man said, 'It was perhaps not his arrival, but his departure. It did not matter.'

I told him the riddle was beyond me. He explained, reluctant as usual, 'Arrivals and departures are illusions. Separation is the only truth.'

I think I suggested, inadvertently, that he was reliving memories. He corrected me severely, 'I am not dreaming but experiencing the truth of the journey, this journey which is sweeping every one of us along.'

His eyes were moist and he went on, 'I saw *him*, he hauled along his baggage and came cheerfully into this lounge. I saw him present his ticket at the counter, and move on for the security check. I saw him, and heard his voice.'

I knew my question was absurd, yet I asked him, 'Did you talk to your son?'

'How could I? I was fortunate enough to hear his voice and laughter. I was grateful for that much, for dividing us was *time*.'

'Didn't that make you sad?'

'It did. But then who is whose child, whose father? We meet during this journey, we love and grieve. That is our lot, this journey and this twilight in which we wait.'

The twilight darkened, and the pollen-eaters and the honey-suckers came back to nest. The beetles hugged leaf stems, and slept. The afterglow of dusk tinted the clouds with saffron. The grass at our feet was wet with dew.

'It is getting late,' he said. 'Let us go.'

We rose from the steps where we sat and crossed the lounge. The old man stopped suddenly at the exit and raised a hand.

'I think I heard one of those telephones ring,' he said.

'You must have imagined it,' I said. The telephones were in disrepair too. They lay under dust and cobwebs, their cables eaten away. But the old man went back to the lounge and picked up a receiver. He pressed it against his ear for a while and then handed it to me, 'Listen.'

I listened. The instrument was dead.

He took the receiver back from me and began listening again. His face grew intent. 'God!' he said. 'They have shot down an airliner near Anchorage. God!'

I seized the receiver and pressed it to my ear. Now a distant voice sounded in the earpiece,'Raghav-ettan, this is me, Ramani.'

'Hello! Hello!' I said raising my voice. 'Who are you, Ramani?'

I do not think my voice reached the other side. Ramani's voice was broken with crying. 'Raghav-ettan, they have shot down the plane. Our Unni is dead.'

My reason said, *disbelieve this voice*, yet I was gripped by its sorrow. This voice which came from nowhere bore the tidings of a child's death. I turned to the old man, 'Who is Ramani, who is Raghavan?'

'I don't know.'

The old man laid his hand on my shoulder, 'We shall never know. This is the journey, the distance. Grieve!'

I found myself trying to make sense of it, futilely. Ramani was Raghav-ettan's sister, living with her husband in Detroit or Minneapolis. Their son Unni was dead. Ramani's sorrow travelled through the withered cables, and sought her brother amidst the ruins of the airport. I had to speak to her.

'Ramani! Ramani!' I screamed into the mouthpiece. 'Can you hear me?'

There was no sound at the other end, yet I said, 'May God's peace be upon Unni. May God protect you.'

In knowledge, in aged quietude, the old man took my hand and led me outside. It was when we were at the door that I saw the large mole on his cheek. It was curious that I had not noticed it before. I stood still, gazing at it.

'My father too had a mole like that,' I said, 'on his cheek.'

'Did he?'

'Not only that, and I am aware of it only now, you resemble my father a good deal.'

'Is that so? Well, coincidences. Let us leave.'

We stepped out onto the grass into the glow of the fireflies and went our separate ways.

*

The next day a great storm kept me from the airport. When I went back the day after I did not find the old man. Now I imagined that I had indeed begun to experience his solitude. I sat on the broken steps and rested my feet on the moist carpet of grass. The pendent nests in the *konnas* had blown away in the storm. The pollen-eaters and the honey-suckers had perished. On the rickety roof of the lounge I thought I heard the chirping of sparrows. I went into the lounge to look for them, but found nothing on the roof. Instead there was the happy chatter of a traveller, his laughter.

God, give me the strength to describe it. I saw one of my own journeys, I saw my own youthful self, an expectant traveller, full of the optimism of adventure. Terror seized me, and unable to bear it, I turned and fled. I found myself in the refuge of a toilet and in its dim and stained mirror I looked into my face. It had become an old face, and on its left cheek was a mole, the old man's mole, my father's mole. I hoped it was an illusion and that I could wash it away. I turned the tap in the basin though I knew that the pipes were long dry. And then from that disused tap a stream of water issued. I caught the water in my palms, and instead of splashing it on my face, drank it reverently. I was certain that the miraculous spring was the stream of the Ganga, the sacred water of the wayfaring pilgrim.

A great tiredness came over me. I listened to the noises in the lounge, and still heard my youthful chatter. The voice changed now to that of my son, and then to that of my father. Arrivals and departures overlapped, mine, my son's and my father's . I stretched my feeble hands again to collect the miraculous water.

I peeped out of the cracked windows. In the dying twilight, like a benediction, I saw them looming over the airport: soft and noiseless ships, flying vessels without arrogance or power. The old man's airplanes! Gently they flew down and landed among the gold-green *konna* bushes.

Going Back

The house where my sister and I lived was on top of a hill, and uncle Kandunni's house was in the valley below, a sprawling feudal manor in whose gentle decay the old man had lived alone. My sister Savitri says that he might have lived a few years longer had not the land reforms dispossessed him, but I do not believe this, having witnessed our old kinsman's strange passing. Uncle Kandunni's estate was taken over by his former tenants, but he bore no grudge against them or against the new law which abolished feudal possession. He was an uncomplaining witness, and had nothing against the peasants turning tenure into proprietorship, but he wondered if that alone met the ends of justice.

'These reforms only settle the account of our *karma*,' uncle Kandunni said. 'We neglect the right of the earth itself.'

When I recounted this to Savitri she said that uncle Kandunni had become senile. I did not think it improbable, yet old ties bound me to uncle Kandunni, memories of my childhood when he taught me the Lord's litany, and I frequently trekked down to the valley to listen to his mysterious utterances.

I remember his last illness, and my anxiety over the state of neglect he lived in. The house had more space than a sick old man could fill, the yard was unswept and little beetles burrowed into its moist upper layers and hauled away balls of mud and moss. And rats scurried about in the house without let or hindrance.

'You need a help, uncle,' I said, 'someone to stay with you.'

Uncle Kandunni surveyed the walls and the ceiling from the couch where he lay, and smiled.

'Not really,' he said. 'That would interfere with them.'

I had an impulse to ask him who they were, but was deterred by my unreasoning reverence for the old man. In these years I have pondered the question: who were *they*? Incarnations of the vital force, deities who attended on lives of grace as they drew to a close, mystic beings who assumed the shape of rat and beetle and dust and moss, who spoke in the chirp of the squirrel on the pomegranate and the rustle of the wind in the palm? As I sat near his bed we could hear the rats gnawing inside the wooden chest, a neurotic grind which seemed to put uncle Kandunni at ease. He was attentive to every sound and sight, he watched with concern the spider spinning overhead, and turned his eyes away for fear his observing should disturb its weave. For him everything was moving towards fullness, an orchestration of many melodies, each perfected by a lifetime of just *karma*. Nothing needed be interfered with, and nothing could be. In this awareness uncle Kandunni rested.

*

The old manor was once full with people—cousins, in-laws, nephews, all of whom had left the ancestral home and scattered to far cities never to come back. And uncle Kandunni's only son, Kunjuraman Kutty, enlisted as a soldier. When that happened, I remember I consoled him, 'Don't worry, uncle. It is peace time, and I do not expect military action in the near future.'

Uncle Kandunni took in my words in a strange and disinterested listening.

'If the political situation worsens,' I went on, 'we can always persuade Kunjuraman Kutty to resign.'

I recall those words of mine, their irrelevance and absurdity.

'Do you remember Gopalakrishnan,' he asked me, 'Gopalakrishnan the astrologer?'

'Yes. I do.'

'You will probably never remember him the way I do.' He paused to reminisce and continued, 'Gopalakrishnan wore a tuft of hair, and I saw his tuft turn luminous.'

As it happened often during our conversations, my sense of reason dimmed, and I sank into the comfort of my old kinsman's mystery. I listened to his story of the luminous tuft and believed it. I convinced myself that the planets' orbits could seep down to the seer and tinge his tuft with cosmic fire.

'Gopalakrishnan drew my son's horoscope to perfection,' uncle Kandunni said, 'nothing has been unforeseen. But it is war I am thinking of.'

Uncle Kandunni did not go on to explain what he thought of war, yet his words, strange and persuasive, led me to contemplate the epic wars of each age, of the ancient covenant which made a father send his only son into battle. Kunjuraman Kutty died fighting.

I went down to the house in the valley to console my kinsman. He was meditating when I entered. But he woke quietly and conversed calmly with me.

'Gopalakrishnan's chart has not gone wrong,' he said. 'It is the planets that have swung into aberrant ellipses. They are afflicted by ancient sorrows. It was with such sorrowing that Gopalakrishnan's tuft glowed. I was witness to it.'

I tried to recreate within myself the experience of those sorrowful ellipses, to see the grieving plumes of the planets as they orbited the skies and shared their grief with the seer below. My contemplation was disturbed by the scurrying of rats. 'Uncle,' I said, 'they are all over the place.'

'Let them be.'

The noise of small teeth gnawing relentlessly was difficult to bear.

'Shall I bring you a cat?' I asked.

'There is no need. They will go away when the time comes and they need no persuading.'

*

When I visited him two days later, the rats had gone. I then looked at uncle Kandunni's book shelves with precognition: the books had vanished, and termites, multitudes of them, were licking away the last remnants of pulp. Uncle Kandunni looked up at me and smiled, 'Look at the way history ends. Eaten up by termites.'

I looked through the window into the corridor. The farm implements, ancient and disused, were in a state of sudden rust. Their metal rusted, while their wood was beset by termites; they were disintegrating even as I watched. A stupor came over me. Uncle Kandunni woke me with his touch. He said, 'I sorrow for my son. This rust and crumbling is my penance for war.'

After a while he recovered his composure. He surveyed the dust of metal and wood, and said with a smile, 'The earth is getting back her rights. Of course it will mean more dispossession.'

Uncle Kandunni looked up at the ceiling. The iron nails struck in the teak girders were coming loose.

'Don't be alarmed,' uncle Kandunni said. 'It is crumbling. I shall do nothing to stop it, I shall stand aside.'

The riddle distressed me, what was my kinsman standing aside from? As though reading my thoughts uncle Kandunni said, 'From metal, from mining. God, I renounce them!'

Uncle Kandunni looked out at the setting sun. His eyes were eager, full of another sun that would rise beyond this sunset, a sun that would renew and heal.

'The earth is becoming aware,' he said.

Golden twilight filled the banana plantation. The flowers at the end of banana bunches opened their pods of honey.

'Come with me into the garden,' uncle Kandunni said. His steps faltered as he walked, but a great joy was on him, as though he was levitating. The squirrels had come for the honey, and to them he said in love, 'Spare me some, my children.'

One pod of honey was enough, there was no need to mine and smelt. There was no need to let the magnets distract the flow of subtle life fluids, there was no need to split the radiant elements. In the benign twilight uncle Kandunni plucked a pod and sucked the honey.

'Now look out,' he said. 'A leaf will fall.'

I waited as if for a miracle. A wind blew through the twilight's gold, and the leaves shivered. There amidst the leaves was one that was ripe for falling, one whose time had come. And it floated down into uncle Kandunni's outstretched hands.

'What grace!' he said, overcome. 'It floated down by itself, I did not have to hurt the twig.'

The right leaf, the renunciant's supper, the gentle eucharist of passing. Uncle Kandunni ate the leaf, in an exquisite ritual that atoned for the primordial hunts of his race.

'It is accomplished,' uncle Kandunni said. 'It is time for me to go.'

'Go where, uncle?'

'Away from here. Don't you see that the rust and termites have overcome?'

Crazily, I found myself asking, 'Has the earth got back its rights?'

Uncle Kandunni smiled, 'Yes, it has.'

I led him back into the house and put him to bed. I bid him rest and returned home.

The next morning my sister Savitri told me of a strange dream she had. She dreamt that uncle Kandunni had turned to fragrant dust on his bed. 'I am disturbed,' she said. 'Go and see him.'

I looked down into the valley and fancied uncle Kandunni's trees appeared greener. I went down the footpath and entered the old house. I looked at the scene before me, sick in the knowledge that Savitri's dream had come true. The bed was untenanted, and on it was scattered a fistful of dust, golden and fragrant like *sandal*. My reason struggled in vain to assert itself. I told myself, without conviction, that uncle Kandunni must have gone visiting his cousins in the next village. Then I was aware of the enormous dissolution around me, the soft gyration of the elements, the dance of particles. The old house was collapsing like a giant canopy of floss.

I rushed out into the garden, and stood sad amidst the joys of the triumphant earth. Then fell a merciful rain, like the water offering for the departed.

The Blessing of the Wild-Fowl

In the basement of our country house there is a disused room where bygone elders of the family had worshipped diverse deities: serpent-gods, the primordial monkey and Garuda, the vehicle of Vishnu. Our house rested on pillars of ageing teak and brooded over this warmth of worship. In it lived the two of us. The other occupant was an old hen I named 'Spotted Dove'.

In my loneliness I often talked to her. 'Spotted Dove,' I would say, 'I see a great sadness in your face.' She would make gentle noises in response, and walk after me, her gait heavy and matronly. I would scatter grains of rice for her which she sometimes pecked and swallowed and at other times abandoned in delicate caprice. I would ask her, 'Spotted Dove, aren't you hungry?'

There was one memory which returned to me insistently, of my days in the city. I had gone to the poultry shop to buy fresh chicken. The shopkeeper strangled the birds with perfect economy, and like an expert surgeon knifed apart leg and wing and breast. In a cage of wire-mesh behind him a brood of chickens sat, drooping.

'I hope these birds are not ill?' I remarked.

'Of course not,' said the shopkeeper. 'They are healthy. I buy them from the state farm, where they are inoculated against the epidemic.'

'Why then do they droop, their feathers ruffled?'

'They sleep.'

'Sleep?'

'They escape the fear of death. They don't want to watch me slaughtering.'

Today I am struck by a similarity in my own experience. My days in the country home were spent in reading and contemplation. The *Gita* and *Katha Upanishad* were the two texts I went over time and again. The immortality promised by the *Gita* failed to console me, the God of the *Gita* seemed to be evading responsibility for the pains He created. Inconclusive too was the *Katha's* long discourse on Death. At the end of each reading I went to sleep.

To return to my conversation with the shopkeeper: 'You spoke of the state poultry farm, didn't you?' I asked him.

'Yes, I did.'

'Where is that?'

'It is in the suburbs, beyond Govandi.'

'A big farm, I suppose?'

'Quite big. It occupies five hectares.'

'That is a lot of space for the chickens to graze in.'

The shopkeeper smiled darkly in his knowledge of the mystery of chickens. He said, 'Foraging days are over for those chickens. They are all in cages, the farm's space is for human employees. The birds themselves are not allowed to move. You know movement toughens the muscles and makes for bad meat.'

'Prisoners for life, aren't they?'

'Yes, if you look at it that way. The fate of the laying hens is even worse. They are bred to lay eggs, which they do all their lives. They do so without mating with roosters, without knowing love.'

'And what happens when they stop laying?'

'They become meat too.'

Half the chickens sleep, unmoving, in cages, I said to myself *the other half lay eggs all their lives, and yet become meat*. I asked,'How many birds are there on the farm?'

'A hundred thousand, at a rough reckoning.'

'If the epidemic infects one bird...'

'You forget what I told you just now. The farm birds are inoculated. It is only the chickens in the country houses that fall ill.'

In the farm beyond Govandi the chickens multiplied, in slavery and in health, and were brought into the city shops, where they readied themselves for death through unnatural sleep, unconsoled by the *Katha's* discourse, their lives spent without movement of limb or the knowledge of love.

'Spotted Dove,' I told my hen one day, 'such is the tragic destiny of your clan.'

She pecked at a grain dispiritedly, then walked out into the yard, raking the loose soil with her feet.

*

I rarely had visitors, preferring to be left alone, yet there were friends whose occasional intrusions cheered me. Unnikrishnan was one such. He visited me one day, armed with his shotgun.

'Nice to see you, Unni,' I said, 'but why the gun?'

'To take you out of your stagnation at gunpoint,' he laughed. 'Now, Bhaskar-ettan, let us go.'

'Where?'

'To the Nelliyampathi mountains.'

'To hunt? Leave me out.'

Unnikrishnan raised me by my shoulder and sat me on the bed, he said, 'Reading books in bed, day and night. What kind of existence is this?'

'Not much of an existence, I admit.'

'Then get up, Bhaskar-ettan, and get ready. If you don't want to shoot, you don't have to. But breathe in the fresh air of Nelliyampathi.'

Unnikrishnan was a great persuader. We walked out over the fields and across the river, we climbed the hills towards Nelliyampathi. Soon we were on the blue and humid mountain. The cane creepers lay around us in immense tangles, from the high canopy of forest trees rose the dithyramb of cicadas. An occasional black monkey leapt across the arching branches with high-pitched shrieks.

'Do you shoot the monkey, Unni?' I asked

'Oh, no! He is the descendant of Hanuman, sacred to Lord Rama!'

So the monkey was free, only a few of his tribe being bred in captivity. Certain creatures seemed to be protected in nature's scheme of things. It did not make sense in terms of sin and grace.

We walked into a clearing. A little stream sparkled across. We stopped to drink, when suddenly, frightened by our movement, a flight of peacocks rose into the air, dazzling us with spreads of turquoise. I was afraid that Unnikrishnan might shoot them down.

'No, Bhaskar-ettan,' Unnikrishnan said. 'The peacock is sacred to Subrahmanya, it is the god's vehicle.'

The peacock was protected, too, like the monkey.

'What about the tiger?' I asked. 'Have you shot tigers?'

'I am scared of tigers. Moreover there is a ban on hunting them.'

So, here was another favoured species. We left the clearing and entered the forest again.

'We haven't seen snakes,'I said.

'Why, do you like them?'

'Mm.'

'This forest is full of snakes, hamadryads.'

The vision of the royal serpent rising out of grass and reed overwhelmed me, its hood spread and branded with the Lord's insignia, an ancient palm raised against the arrogance of creatures. I thought of the conflict between the two wives of the legendary sage. One was to mother the tribe of serpents, and the other, Aruna and Garuda. The mother of Aruna hatched his egg before time, and he came out with no limbs below his waist. He became the Sun's charioteer, seated forever legless. He became the god of dawn. His brother Garuda was born in the fullness of time, a great eagle with magical powers. Garuda and the serpents feuded, in the *karmic* maze of sin and retribution, through long and bloody ages. Such conflict seemed to be the lot of sentient beings, while above its tumult blew the breezes with the deeper awareness inert matter was heir to. Once in a long while a solitary bird or beast would understand this serenity.

'No game seems to come our way,' Unnikrishnan said.

'Then let us rest for a while.'

It was past noon. We sat down on the grass and opened the packages of food we had brought with us. As we sat, a flock of birds of bright red and black and yellow plumage flew in and settled on the tree tops above us. Unnikrishnan leapt up. 'Bhaskar-ettan, wild-fowl!'

The ancient forebears of domestic chickens, whom nature had spared incarceration in Govandi, whose wings still had the power of flight, and whose vibrant muscles had not been degraded by the needs of the epicure. Unnikrishnan took aim.

'Stop, Unni, stop!' I cried. Taken aback by the urgency of my words, Unnikrishnan lowered his gun.

'What is it, Bhaskar-ettan?'

'Leave the wild-fowl alone.'

'What has come over you?'

'Let us not harm the wild-fowl!' I said. I had decided that my love would be the protection of the wild-fowl, ancestors of my Spotted Dove, a clan with no divine protection.

'I shall not shoot,' Unnikrishnan said, 'if you feel so strongly about it.' He laid the gun on the grass and sat down beside it. The sun dipped westward and the mountain breeze cooled.

'Unni,' I said, 'let us go home.'

'Let us. But we shall have chicken for supper.'

I thought of my Spotted Dove following me, trusting and secure, pecking and discarding grains of rice. 'Tonight I shall give you a different supper,' I said.

'What kind of supper?'

'Gruel and coconut juice and steamed peas.'

Unnikrishnan laughed, 'Ascetic as usual!'

By sundown we were back home. Spotted Dove was in the yard, waiting for me. She bent her head in greeting, crooned, fluttered round me and led me into the house.

'She is telling you something,' Unnikrishnan said.

'Yes.'

Spotted Dove led me to the basement. There in a corner was an egg.

'Spotted Dove,' I said 'you have kept your love a secret!'

I returned to where Unnikrishnan was and made supper. After we had eaten the gruel and peas, Unnikrishnan went home.

*

Spotted Dove laid another egg the next day, and then stopped. I felt her, she was warm for the brooding. I tended her as she prepared to hatch the egg. I told her of my encounter with her wild ancestors in Nelliyampathi. She listened with deep understanding.

On the fifteenth day a strange impatience seized me. I went down to the basement and pulled out an egg from beneath her and pressed it to my ear. Inside the shell there was noise and movement. I cracked the shell open. Spotted Dove looked on in alarm. From the splintered shell there emerged, luminous and mystic, a winged human form, with no limbs below the waist. The legless Aruna, the Sun's charioteer! I put him down in front of his mother and said, 'Spotted Dove, forgive me. Mine was the impatience of love, and I, the blundering human, have intruded into the genesis of birds. But before long he will rise into the skies to take the reins of the chariot. Now brood on the other egg.'

I went back to bed. That night I saw a blinding trajectory of light rise up to the heavens. I saw it, and so did the wild-fowl of Nelliyampathi.

My days passed in lucid wakefulness and gentle dreaming. I went down to the basement on the twenty-first day. Spotted Dove, brimming over with the caring warmth of motherhood, was getting ready to peck the egg open. I stood by in humility, waiting for the incarnation.

'Spotted Dove,' I said, 'do you realize who this is?'

Soft light emanated from the egg and filled the basement. A new Garuda stepped out, cleansed of the long ages of conflict. *He will no longer hunt down his serpent brethren, but go instead in search of Amrit, the elixir of eternal life.* I whispered the vedic prayer, *Mrityoma Amritham Gamaya, lead us from death to immortality.*

That night another trajectory of light signified the second ascent. The next morning Spotted Dove followed me round the house, pecking at grains of rice.

And the mountain winds blew down on our house, with the love of the wild-fowl of Nelliyampathi.

After the Hanging

As Vellayi-appan set out on his journey the sound of ritual mourning rose from his hut, and from Ammini's hut, and beyond those huts the village listened in grief. Vellayi-appan was going to Cannanore. Had they the money, each one of them would have accompanied him on the journey, it was as though he was journeying for the village. Vellayi-appan now passed the last of the huts and took the long ridge across the paddies. The crying receded behind him. From the ridge he stepped on pasture land across which the footpath meandered.

Gods, my lords, Vellayi-appan cried within himself.

The black palms rose on either side and the wind clattered in their fronds. The wind, ever so familiar, was strange this day—the gods of his clan and departed elders were talking to him through the wind-blown fronds. Slung over his shoulder was a bundle of cooked rice, and its wet seeped through the threadbare cloth into his arm. His wife had bent long over the rice, kneading it for the journey, and as she had cried the while her tears had soaked into the sour curd. Vellayi-appan walked on. The railway station was four miles away. Further down the path he saw Kuttihassan walking towards him. Kuttihassan stepped aside from the path, in tender reverence.

'Vellayi,' said Kuttihassan.

'Kuttihassan,' replied Vellayi-appan.

That was all, just two words, two names, yet it was like a long colloquy, in which there was lament and consolation. *O Kuttihassan,* said the unspoken words, *I have a debt to pay you, fifteen silvers.*

Let that not burden you, O Vellayi, on this journey.

Kuttihassan, I may never be able to pay you, never after this.

We consign our unredeemed debts to God's keeping. Let His will be done.

I burn within myself, my life is being prised away.

May the Prophet guard you on this journey, may the gods bless you, your gods and mine.

The dithyramb of the gods was now a torrent in the palms. Vellayi-appan passed Kuttihassan and walked on. Four miles to go to the train station. Again, an encounter on the way. Neeli, the laundress, with her bundles of washing. She too stepped aside reverentially.

'Vellayi-appan,' she said.

'Neeli,' said Vellayi-appan.

Just these two words, and yet between them the abundant colloquy. Vellayi-appan walked on.

The footpath joined the mud road, and Vellayi-appan looked for the milestone and continued on his way. Presently he came to where the rough-hewn track descended into the river. Across the river, beyond a rise and a stretch of sere grass, was the railway. Vellayi-appan stepped onto the sands, then into the knee-deep water. Schools of little fish, gleaming silver, rubbed against his calves and swam on. As he reached the middle of the river Vellayi-appan was overwhelmed by the expanse of water, it reminded him of sad and loving rituals, of the bathing of his father's corpse, of his little son swimming in the river's currents; all this he remembered, and pausing on the river bank wept in memory.

He reached the railway station and made his way to the ticket counter and with great care undid the knot in the corner of his unsewn cloth to take out the money for the fare.

'Cannanore,' Vellayi-appan said. The clerk behind the counter pulled out a ticket, franked it, and tossed it towards him. *One stage in my journey is over*, thought Vellayi-appan. He secured the ticket in the corner of his unsewn cloth and crossing over to the platform sat on a bench, waiting patiently for his train. He watched the sun sink and the palms darken far away, and the birds flit homewards. Vellayi-appan remembered walking with his son to the fields at sundown, he remembered how his son had looked up at the birds in wonder. Then he remembered himself as a child, holding onto his father's little finger, and walking down the same fields. Two images, but between them as between two reticent words, an abundance of many things. Soon another aged traveller came over and sat beside him on the bench.

'Going to Coimbatore, are you?' the stranger asked.

'Cannanore,' Vellayi-appan said.

'I go to Coimbatore.'

'Is that so?'

'The Cannanore train will be at ten in the night.'

'Is that so?'

'What work do you do in Cannanore?'

'Nothing much.'

'Just travelling, are you?'

The stranger's converse, inane and rasping, tensed round Vellayi-appan like a hangman's noose. Once you left the village and walked over the long ridge, it was a world full of strangers, and their disinterested words were like a multitude of nooses. The train to Coimbatore came, and the old stranger rose and left. Vellayi-appan was again alone on the bench. He had no desire to untie the bundle of rice, instead he kept a hand on the threadbare wrap, he felt its moisture. He sat thus and slept. And dreamt. In his dream he called out, 'Kandunni, my son!'

The noise of the train woke Vellayi-appan, and he scrambled up. He felt for the ticket in the knot of his cloth, and jostling feebly through the crowd, sought a way in.

'This is first class, O elder.'

'Is that so?'

He peered into the next compartment.

'This is reserved.'

'Is that so?'

'Try further down, O elder.'

The voice of strangers.

Vellayi-appan got into a compartment where there was no sitting space left. He could barely stand. *I shall stand, I don't need to sleep, this night my son sits awake*. The rhythm of the train changed with the changing layers of the earth, the fleeting trackside lamps, sand banks, trees. Long ago he had travelled in a train, but that was in the day. This was a night train. It sped through the tunnel of darkness, whose arching walls were painted with dim murals..

The day had not broken when he reached Cannanore. The bundle of kneaded rice still hung from his shoulder, oozing its wet. He passed through the gate into the station yard, the dark now livened with the first touch of dawn. The horse-cart men clumsily parked together, did not accost him.

Vellayi-appan asked them, 'Which is the way to the jail?'

Someone laughed. *Here is an old man asking the way to the jail at daybreak*. Someone laughed again, *O elder, all you have to do is to steal, they will take you there*. The converse of strangers tightened round his neck. Vellayi-appan suffocated.

Then someone told him the way and Vellayi-appan began to walk. The sky lightened to the orchestration of crows cawing.

At the gate of the jail a guard stopped him, 'What brings you here this early?'

Vellayi-appan shrank back like a child, nervous. Then slowly he undid the corner of his cloth and took out a crumpled and yellowing piece of paper.

'What is that?' the guard enquired.

Vellayi-appan handed him the paper, the guard glanced through it without reading.

Vellayi-appan said, 'My child is here.'

'Who told you to come so early?' the guard asked, his voice irritable and harsh. 'Wait till the office is open.'

Then his eyes fell on the paper again, and became riveted to its contents. His face, hostile a while ago, softened in sudden compassion.

'Tomorrow, is it?' the guard asked, almost consoling.

'I don't know. It is all written down there.'

The guard read and re-read the order. 'Yes,' he said, 'it's tomorrow morning at five.'

Vellayi-appan's eyes opened wide, 'Is that so?'

'Sit down and rest yourself, O elder.'

Vellayi-appan nodded in acknowledgement, and slumped on a bench at the entrance of the jail. There he waited for the dark sanctum to open.

'O elder, may I offer you a cup of tea?' the guard asked solicitously.

'No.'

My son has not slept this night, and not having slept, would not have woken. Neither asleep nor awake, how can he break his fast this morning? Vellayi-appan's hand rested on the bundle of rice. *My son, this rice was kneaded by your mother for me. I saved it during all the hours of my travel, and brought it here. Now this is all I have to bequeath to you.* The rice inside the threadbare wrap, food of the traveller, turned stale. Outside, the day brightened. The day grew hot.

The offices opened, and staid men took their places behind the tables. In the prison yard there was the grind of a parade. The prison came alive. The officers got to work, bending over yellowing papers in tedious scrutiny. From behind the tables, and where the column of the guards waited in formation, came rasping orders, words of command. Nooses without contempt or vengeance, gently strangulating the traveller. The day grew hotter.

Someone told him, *sit down and wait*. Vellayi-appan sat down, he waited. After a wait, the length of which he could not reckon, a guard led him into the corridors of the prison. The corridors were cool with the damp of the prison. *We're here, O elder.*

Behind the bars of a locked cell stood Kandunni. He looked at his father like a stranger, through the awesome filter of a mind that could no longer receive nor give consolation. The guard opened the door and let Vellayi-appan into the cell. Father and son stood facing each other, petrified. Then Vellayi-appan leaned forward to take his son in an embrace. From Kandunni came a cry that pierced beyond hearing, and when it died down, Vellayi-appan said, 'My son!'

'Father!' said Kandunni.

Just these words, but in them father and son communed in the fullness of sorrow.

Son, what did you do?

I have no memory, father.

Son, did you kill?

I have no memory.

It does not matter, my son, there is nothing to remember anymore.

Will the guards remember?

No, my son.

Father, will you remember my pain?

Then again the cry that pierced beyond hearing issued from Kandunni, *Father don't let them hang me.*

'Come out, O elder,' the guard said, 'the time is over.'

Vellayi-appan came away and the door clanged shut.

One last look back, and Vellayi-appan saw his son like a stranger met during a journey. Kandunni was peering through the bars as a traveller might through the window of a hurtling train.

Vellayi-appan wandered idly around the jail. The sun rose to its zenith, then began the climb down. *Will my son sleep this night?* The night came, and moved to dawn again. Within the walls Kandunni still lived.

Vellayi-appan heard the sound of bugles at dawn, little knowing that this was death's ceremonial. But the guard had told him that it was at five in the morning and though he wore no watch, Vellayi-appan knew the time with the peasant's unerring instinct.

*

Vellayi-appan received the body of his son from the guards like a midwife a baby.

O elder, what plans do you have for the funeral?

I have no plans.

Don't you want the body?

Masters, I have no money.

Vellayi-appan walked along with the scavengers who pushed the trolley carrying the body. Outside the town, over the deserted marshes, the vultures wheeled patiently. Before the scavengers filled the pit Vellayi-appan saw his son's face just once more. He pressed his palm on the cold forehead in blessing.

After the last shovelful of earth had levelled the pit, Vellayi-appan wandered in the gathering heat and eventually came to the beach. He had never seen the ocean before. Then he became aware of something cold and wet in his hands, the rice his wife had kneaded for his journey. Vellayi-appan undid the bundle.He scattered the rice on the sand, in sacrifice and requiescat. From the crystal reaches of the sunlight, crows descended on the rice, like incarnate souls of the dead come to receive the offering.

The River

Parameswaran's daily bath in the river was an elaborate ritual. After scrubbing and washing himself, he would stay in the water a long while, seated on the sands of the shallows. The little girl, Nangema Kutty, who invariably bathed nearby would often ask him, 'Uncle Parameswaran, haven't you finished your bath yet?'

'I have, in a sense,' he would reply. 'In another, I haven't.'

'That is a riddle.'

Parameswaran would smile when she taunted him thus. On certain days he would sit facing the source of the river, and on other days in the direction of the current. The naughty girl noticed this too, and demanded an explanation one day.

'Have patience, my child,' Parameswaran said. 'You will understand when you are grown.'

'How grown?'

'When you grow as old as your grandmother.'

'That is a long while to go. Can't you tell me before that?'

'I shall tell you if you are that impatient,' Parameswaran said. 'It is this, that all of us someday have to flow down the river.'

'Me too?'

'No one escapes.'

'I don't want to float away.'

Parameswaran watched the flow of the river, aware of its sensuous ripples around his body.

'Why don't you want to float away?' he asked her.

'I am afraid.'

'That is a child's fear. You won't be afraid when you are grown.'

Nangema Kutty finished her bath and changed. That day Parameswaran sat facing the source.

'That reminds me,' Nangema Kutty said looking at him, 'you haven't told me why you face a particular direction.'

Reluctantly Parameswaran spoke, 'I told you that all of us float away. It being so, we should know all about the river, where it springs from and where it flows to.'

'Have you found out, uncle Parameswaran?'

'Little by little, with each passing day.'

'When will you know the whole truth?'

Parameswaran sat looking at his own body for a long time and finally said, 'In good time.'

'You are crazy, uncle Parameswaran.'

Giggling, Nangema Kutty climbed out of the river.

*

Years passed. Nangema Kutty was married off to another village, and Parameswaran had no one to talk to about the river. It was just as well, Parameswaran thought, these relationships obstruct the great flow.

Now Parameswaran stopped turning towards the source. *I have learnt all about the source,* he told himself, *what remains to be known is the sea.*

One day there was an unexpected bather, Krishnan-*vaidyan*, the medicine man from the next village.

'I seldom see you bathe at this spot, O *vaidyan*,' Parameswaran said as the medicine man entered the water.

'I am on my way to visit a patient,' Krishnan-*vaidyan* said. 'Seeing the river I couldn't resist the temptation of a dip.'

'It will do you good.'

The medicine man finished his bath and went his way.

'Goodbye, Parameswaran-ettan,' he said. 'Take care of yourself.'

On his way back, after two hours, Krishnan-*vaidyan* found Parameswaran still sitting in the water.

'What are you doing?' the medicine man asked. 'Haven't you finished your bath?'

Parameswaran merely turned a blank smile on his friend.

The medicine man continued, 'You are not young anymore. Too much of this will make you ill.'

Saying this, Krishnan-*vaidyan* resumed his journey. Parameswaran continued to sit in the water. For the first time in all these years, he sensed his feet grow light, as though the river was washing away old encrustations. As the river flowed away with the gross elements, a trail of awareness seemed to stem from his extremities and follow them on their journey. Soon he could sense the estuary, he felt he was sitting with his feet dipped in the far ocean.

It was noon and there were no bathers in the river.

Parameswaran was relieved. Around him the waters grew vibrant, sentient. They washed away more of his gross matter, patiently undoing each successive layer. When his calves and thighs were pared away, his knowledge of the sea became larger. A sensuous fatigue came over him when he felt the river work on his hands and shoulders, and reach out to his neck. When all that dismembered matter flowed away he began sensing the current with his subtle spine. Joy flowered in his brain as a thousand-petalled lotus.

Parameswaran was now the lotus afloat in the river. How long had he waited for this flowering! In the radiance of the petals, in the pure knowledge of the flower, Parameswaran watched the flower itself dissolve.

The river became experience, it became knowledge and light. When the last petal dissolved, Parameswaran knew the whole of the river, and he laughed from mountain to sea.

THE DIVERSIONS

Spring Thunder

Government officers the world over revel in sloppiness and sloth; their strength lies in their backlog of paper work. So it was that terror gripped the clerks of the *tahsildar's* office, when they discovered that someone had broken in at night and cleared all the pending correspondence and brought the accounts up-to-date.

Ten days later another attack was reported from the office of a village council. The nocturnal assailant had spruced up the files, dusted the furniture and dissolved the clots of ink in the long-dried bottles. The attendant who opened the office in the morning saw that even the clock had been wound and its hands set. The clock had idled for several months and the sight of it running was too much for the attendant. He died of shock.

This death caused great alarm in the bureaucracy. The attacks were repeated in the days that followed, and more and more offices streamlined. A hunt began for the assailant.

The most dramatic attack occurred in the District Treasury. The pension papers of a dozen government employees retired for years were brought up-to-date. The old men were grateful but the clerks were aghast. The clerks' terror was heightened by the Thoughts of Sir Tottenham, which the assailant had inscribed on the walls in large characters. Sir Tottenham was the legendary civil servant who had invented the delay-free filing system.

By now Intelligence had identified the assailant. He was a young South Indian Brahmin by the name of Tatachari Venkatachari. Secret servicemen, aided by distraught clerks, combed the jungles for the guerrilla, but he was elusive, surfacing at will and choosing his place of strike. The organization of international stenographers, the Shortinform, lauded the insurrection in its official journal and described it as Spring Thunder.

The hunt was intensified, but Tatachari Venkatachari outran his pursuers. He was the fastest stenographer in the whole of South Asia. The bureaucracy was sunk in gloom. The state threatened to wither away.

Then the most unexpected thing happened. Tatachari Venkatachari's insurrection collapsed abruptly. Tatachari Venkatachari reported back for work.

He had exhausted his leave, and leave rules for an extremist steno were as immutable as the laws of shorthand or accountancy. With the collapse of the revolution, the bureaucracy re-established its hegemony, and the clerks sat over accumulations of unattended correspondence in contentment. The revolution passed into legend.

The Progressive Classic

The lovers sat on the deserted riverside, the full moon above them. He held her close. Their lips met.

'Darling,' she said, 'there is something on my mind.'

'Tell me, precious,' he said.

'Have you read Karl Marx's *Das Kapital?*'

'I haven't. I have been wanting to.'

He began undoing her blouse.

'Have patience,' she said. 'Let us read *Kapital*. I have brought it with me.'

He took his hand off her and said, 'As you wish.'

They lit a lamp by the riverside and began reading

'..,..'

After many months, when they had finished the four volumes of *Kapital*, he resumed his petting.

'I love you,' she said.

The moon shone over them.

*

Post Script: *Readers are requested to get hold of the four volumes of* Das Kapital *and fill in the blanks. If they do so, this little story will become the lengthiest Socialist-realist novel in contemporary literature.*

The Legend

He laid the boulder aside and returned to the city, to write an entrance examination to the bureaucracy. He rose in the service, was decorated, grew old and his teeth came loose. When the last tooth fell he clapped his hands and laughed.

(Strike out the above paragraph and read on).

One morning he asked his chauffeur to fill the tank of his car and prepare to set out.

'Where to, Sir?' the chauffeur asked.

'Drive straight ahead, you dunce,' he said.

The chauffeur drove him through villages and towns, without purpose, the whole day. At night, when they returned home he clapped his hands and laughed.

(Strike out the above paragraph and read on).

He married a girl, made love to her, and made her pregnant. When she delivered he clapped his hands and laughed.

(Strike out and read on).

He became a media celebrity, securing invitations and a round-the-world ticket. From Delhi to Moscow, Frankfurt, London, New York, Tokyo, Hong Kong, Bangkok, and back to Delhi.

As he entered his flat again he clapped his hands and laughed.

He had many pseudonyms, but his real name was Sisyphus.

*

Note on the story: *Kerala legends speak of a character similar to Sisyphus, Naranathu Bhranthan — the mad man of Naranathu. He spent his life rolling a boulder up a cliff, and clapping his hands as he let the boulder roll back.*

The Grand Mughal's Gift

A fishbone got stuck in Emperor Akbar's throat one day. There were no surgeons yet in the Mughal Empire, and the Court Hakim could not get the bone out. So the stork was brought in.

'Take the bone out,' said Akbar. 'You shall be amply rewarded.' The stork bowed and then put its head between the Emperor's jaws. It took the bone out.

'Get lost,' said the Emperor.

'My reward,' the stork reminded him nervously.

'No creature that has peeped into the throat of the Mughal Emperor has ever taken its head out. I have let you emerge unscathed, what reward can be greater than your own head?'

There was little that a stork could do against an Emperor, but what made it feel even more wretched was that the whole story was lifted from Aesop's *Fables*.

The Meteor

Bodhavrata awoke one night from a dream of shooting stars.

He saw a large shadow on the moonlit yard and came out of his house to investigate. He saw a Meteor hovering over his cottage.

He was not cowed down by its size; he reminded himself he was a scholar. He challenged the Meteor, 'Do you know as much mathematics as I do?'

'I know no mathematics,' the Meteor answered.

'Poetics?'

'No poetics either.'

'What good are your then?' Bodhavrata said contemptuously.

The Meteor replied meekly, 'We are an unlettered lot, we the stars of heaven.'

THE SAGA OF DHARMAPURI

O.V. Vijayan

The citizens of Dharmapuri suffer mightily at the hands of their President, a gross tyrant, until the day a benevolent mystic with vast magical powers arrives on the borders of their country. The state of Dharmapuri, it appears, has found a saviour but Siddhartha, the mystic, finds that even his great goodness and magic are in danger of being overpowered by the strength of the dictator's wickedness... Then, quite unexpectedly, he discovers the path he must follow if he is to succeed in his task of setting free the people of Dharmapuri. A glittering extravaganza of myth, allegory, dark humour, scatology, eroticism, mystic insights, and literary innovation, *The Saga of Dharmapuri* firmly establishes O.V. Vijayan in the forefront of contemporary Indian novelists.

"The book is an important landmark in contemporary Indian writing."—*The Indian Post*

THE HOTEL RIVIERA

R.K. Laxman

The arrival of Sabitha, a voluptuous and sensual 'orphan' at the Hotel Riviera, a squalid little flophouse in Bombay, destroys forever the amicable co-existence of its inhabitants.

For a start, Sabitha's presence has a cataclysmic effect on the manager of the hotel, an inhibited small-town person, who is totally unmanned by the glamorous vamp. Madly in love, he begins to come apart mentally and physically when she rejects all his amorous overtures. As the path of true love becomes increasingly rocky, the manager turns morose and hostile towards the other employees and long-term residents of the hotel—Rao, the clerk, a relative of the proprietor, **Achar,** the cook who believes in spoon-down strikes at the least word of criticism, Francis, the liftman and resident snoop, the Major, a gun-waving, alcoholic hotel guest, **Swamiji,** an amazingly incompetent godman and several others—and they in turn gang up against him. Frantic, the manager tries to resolve all his problems at one stroke but only succeeds in adding more chaos to an already hilariously confused situation.

"Laxman's novel is inhabited by ordinary people trapped in ordinary situations, seeking escape-routes into a world more exciting than the one available."

—***Indian Express***

ARJUN

Sunil Gangopadhyay

Arjun thinks he is in love with a beautiful college girl, but he falls prey to the fear that he is wooing someone far above his station. For Arjun is a poor, if brilliant and resourceful, refugee from East Bengal living in a squatter's settlement on the outskirts of Calcutta, whereas the girl he is keen on is the daughter of a wealthy doctor. But his love-life is the least of his problems, he soon discovers, as a crooked landlord and a disreputable factory owner join forces in an attempt to evict the people of Arjun's community from their hard-won land. Arjun now has to choose between fighting alongside the people he has grown up with, against the forces that threaten to engulf them all, or escaping to the safe haven his wealthy Bengali friends are willing to provide. He chooses to fight in a stunning climax to a powerful and sensitively written novel.